Three Exemplary Novels

ALSO TRANSLATED BY SAMUEL PUTNAM

THE INGENIOUS GENTLEMAN DON QUIXOTE DE LA MANCHA

THE PORTABLE RABELAIS

THREE
EXEMPLARY NOVELS

Miguel de Cervantes Saavedra

Translated by Samuel Putnam

MIGUEL DE CERVANTES

Illustrated by Luis Quintanilla

THE VIKING PRESS · NEW YORK · 1950

THIS FIRST EDITION, OF THREE THOUSAND
COPIES, WAS PRINTED FROM TYPE AND FROM
THE ARTIST'S OWN ENGRAVINGS, AND THE
TYPE DESTROYED

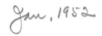

COPYRIGHT 1950 BY THE VIKING PRESS, INC.

PUBLISHED IN SEPTEMBER 1950

PUBLISHED ON THE SAME DAY IN THE DOMINION OF CANADA
BY THE MACMILLAN COMPANY OF CANADA LIMITED

SET IN JANSON AND GOUDY MEDIEVAL TYPES
AND PRINTED IN U.S.A. BY THE VAIL-BALLOU PRESS, INC.

Rinconete and Cortadillo

Man of Glass

The Colloquy of the Dogs

To
Riva Putnam

PUBLISHER'S NOTE

Upon the completion of his great translation of *Don Quixote*, Samuel Putnam, shortly before his death in March 1950, proceeded to translate three of Cervantes' *Novelas Ejemplares*, which are presented for the first time in this volume. The introductory material consists of passages from his unpublished essay on Cervantes and all of his prefatory remarks on these stories.

Table of Contents

Translator's Introduction

Cervantes has left us, besides the *Don Quixote*, another masterly work—the *Exemplary Novels*. Unfortunately, these are little known to American readers though they have had a ponderable effect upon the literature of England and the Continent. There are two translations, one by N. Maccoll, the other by Walter K. Kelly; the former is by far the better of the two, but both have long been out of print and are difficult to procure. This is to be regretted; had they been accessible, these novels would surely have made themselves felt by writers and by students of the art of fiction generally. There are some who see in the *Novelas Ejemplares* Cervantes' most mature production from the point of view of a highly conscious and refined literary artistry.

As a prose writer, master of a beautifully pure and limpid Castilian, Cervantes is the best that the Golden Age has to show, neither Lope de Vega nor Quevedo being comparable to him in this regard. His native style is admirably terse, vigorous, and direct, and reminds one somewhat of Swift's. He has his faults, to be sure. There are signs of haste or careless writing now and then, and there are occasional traces of "fine" writing, possibly due to the Góngora influence; but on the whole he is true to the apothegm that he uses twice in the *Don Quixote*: "*Toda afectación es mala*"—"All affectation is bad."

Three of the best of the *Novelas Ejemplares* are here presented in a new version: "Rinconete and Cortadillo," "Man of Glass," and "The Colloquy of the Dogs." An effort has been made to hold the notes (for some of which I am especially indebted to F. Rodríguez Marín) to that minimum required for intelligibility, the needs of the student of fiction being kept primarily in mind.

"Rinconete and Cortadillo" is a tale of the picaresque and, according to the accounts that have come down to us, indescribably picturesque city of Seville at the turn of the seventeenth century. With a large population representing a hundred or more nationalities and governed by an exceedingly lax and corrupt municipal administration, the town was filled to overflowing with thieves, bandits, lawbreakers of every sort. Disorder was rife. Officers of the law and rogues frequently worked together, while an "espía doble" lent his services to both sides. One chronicler, Luís de Peraza, tells us in his *History of the Imperial City of Seville* that even small boys went armed in imitation of their elders, and thieves' jargon (*germanía*) was almost a common speech, one with which Cervantes was obviously well acquainted. And in the *Miscelanea* of Luís Zapata, a work probably written about the end of the sixteenth century, the following passage will be found:

In Seville there is said to be a brotherhood of thieves, with a prior and consuls who serve as vendors; it has a depository for stolen goods and a chest with three keys in which the loot is kept; from this chest they take what they need to defray expenses and to bribe those who are in a position to help them when they are in trouble. They are very careful to accept only men who are strong and active and old Christians, their membership being limited to the servants of powerful and high-placed individuals, agents of the law; and the first oath to which they swear is that, even though they may be drawn and quartered, they will endure it and will not inform on their companions. And so, when something is missing from the home of a respectable citizen and people say that the devil has taken it, the truth of the matter is that it is not the devil but one of these. That they have a brotherhood is certain, and it has lasted longer than the principality of Venice; for although the law has caught a few unfortunate ones, it has never been able to run down the leader of the gang.

With regard to the religious aspect of the community, Rodríguez Marín has this to say:

To be a thief and serve God at one and the same time is something that is very characteristic of the Spanish, and especially the Andalusian, underworld. "Steal the pig and give the feet to God," as the proverb has it, was a practice common everywhere, and rarely was a bandit caught or slain without medals and scapulars being found upon his chest. I myself have heard and copied down some of the prayers that were used by highwaymen sixty years ago in an effort to render themselves invisible against their armed pursuers.

Out of such a setting Cervantes has drawn vivid types. During his residence there he hardly could have failed to absorb all the color and the movement of the place, and with the true novelist's instinct he has put the experience to good use. He has also doubtless embodied much that he learned in prison. Here is the social-realistic—true to life—side of his art; but in the end there is, as always with Cervantes, a larger implication.

The germ of *Don Quixote* may be discovered in this story. It lies in that contrast, the humorous incongruity, between the world as it is and the world as it ought to be, which constitutes Cervantes' major theme and forms the basis of his finest art. What we have

here, in short, is a close-to-life realism, which in itself will doubtless suffice for many but which holds a deeper meaning for those
who seek it.

The "El Licenciado Vidriera" (literally, "The Licentiate of
Glass" or "The Licentiate Glasscase") is a story concerning which
critical opinion has varied somewhat, but most authorities look
upon it as one of the best of the *Exemplary Novels*. Such distinguished scholars as Marcelino Menéndez y Pelayo and Francisco
A. de Icaza have believed that here Cervantes is merely using the
novel form as an excuse for the stringing together of apothegms—
in other words, for saying things that he wanted said; and, in fact,
the author does seize the opportunity to express himself force-
fully on a number of subjects that are favorites of his: on book-
sellers (publishers) and their treatment of writers, on actors,
dramatists, and the theater, on the state of poetry, and so forth.
It would appear much more likely, however, that his real interest
lay in the theme of madness—which seems to have been something of an obsession with him, as it was with the mature Shake-
speare—and in the bitter ironic twist at the end, with the madman who has regained his sanity being left to starve by a society
that previously has supported him and followed him about and
that now compels him, in order to live, to embrace the life of a
soldier and die on the battlefield.

In a way it is the *Don Quixote* theme again, though not quite
the same, and again the "madness" of the protagonist is ques-
tionable. Though in a short story such as this there is much less
opportunity for the gradual development of character, than in a
long work like the *Don Quixote*, even here the licentiate's madness
is motivated with a certain realism and credibility, with an avoid-
ance of the miraculous. May we not see in Glasscase a Don

Quixote who in place of romances of chivalry has been reading theological tomes and works on moral philosophy? He is the truth teller, the social and moral satirist (for his social satire is motivated always from the moral and religious point of view), who sallies forth to reveal to his fellowmen the lie upon which the existence of nearly everyone is based. The various trades, professions, occupations are in turn subjected to his denuding irony; it is the whole of human society that is under indictment in the sight of Heaven, Plato's heaven of ideals and that of the Christian as well; but in the end it is the idealist himself who is overthrown, just as the Knight of La Mancha was, and once more we are brought face to face with the problem of the world as it is and the world as it ought to be.

Aside from its philosophical implications, the "Man of Glass" is of interest for the autobiographical elements it contains, particularly the reminiscences of Italy (Cervantes, like the hero of the tale, may also have served in Flanders). The young Rodaja's itinerary, the cities he visited, the sights he saw, the wines he drank and the food he ate, may well be a reflection of the author's own experiences. If true, this would confirm the view that Cervantes' acquaintance with Italy was comparatively slight, scarcely going beyond that of a tourist. There will also be found more than one passage that has a light to throw on Cervantes' intellectual and spiritual biography, his attitudes and prejudices, his personal likes and dislikes, his view of his literary contemporaries and of the life that a writer had to lead. When, for instance, we are told that Rodaja carried with him only two volumes, a book containing prayers to Our Lady and a Garcilaso "without notes," are we not perhaps justified in assuming that the author's own pocket library was similarly constituted? It would be in keeping with what we know of Cervantes the devout Catholic and admirer of Garcilaso de la Vega.

On the side of form, this novel presents certain difficulties for the translator which would tempt him to shun the task of rendering it into English. In a number of places the humor is dependent upon word plays, some of which are quite untranslatable while others can only be suggested. But the story impressed this editor as being too good, too important to be omitted, and he has accordingly done his best with it.

Though in reality "The Colloquy of the Dogs" ("El Coloquio de los Perros") stands alone as one of the finest examples of Cervantes' art in the *novela* form, it is supposed to be a story within a story, or rather, an appendage to "The Deceitful Marriage." A sick veteran in the hospital, who is being subjected to the sweating treatment, fancies that he hears the canine conversation outside his window one night and writes it down. It is only natural that the critics should have found an analogy between this piece and the *Golden Ass* of Apuleius; but as one editor, Angel Valbuena y Prat, has pointed out, the two works actually have nothing in common. A comparison with the *Dialogues* of Lucian might seem to be more pertinent—Menéndez y Pelayo has spoken of Cervantes as being in a manner the "disciple and heir" of the Greek writer—but there is a fundamental difference in worldview: Cervantes is the Christian moralist rather than the satirist.

The truth is, "The Colloquy of the Dogs" stands in need of no literary pedigree, and Cervantes might well have written it if Apuleius or Lucian had never lived or he had never read them; for it is woven out of his own distinctive imagination and life experiences. Interior evidence shows that it must have been composed between 1599 and 1609, the likely date being 1603–1604, or prior to the spring of 1605. It was during these early years of the century, from 1601 to 1605, that Valladolid, where the Hospital of the Resurrection is located in the story, became once more the capital of Spain. Cervantes was summoned to Valladolid, in connection with the debt that he owed the crown as a tax gatherer, in 1603, and he moved his family there around 1604. The details regarding the city have been found by modern scholars to be realistically exact, and even the witchcraft episode of Montilla (there is evidence that Cervantes was in Montilla in July 1592 as a commissary) is based upon a historical incident that may be verified from the records of the Inquisition.

In this novel, particularly as regards witchcraft, there is excellent opportunity to study Cervantes' literary method, the way in which he utilized historical and real-life material. The popular sources are clearly discernible; for Cervantes has drawn upon the fund of folk sayings, legends, superstitions, and tales of witches' trials that he acquired while roaming the countryside as an agent of the King. There are other features of the story which have a basis in historical fact. The stealing of meat from the municipal slaughter house is a case in point. In order to prevent such thefts, the records show, special steps had to be taken by the *asistente* of Seville, Don Diego Hurtado de Mendoza. We are also given a tantalizing glimpse of student life in Cervantes' time, in the course of which the author takes occasion to pay a high tribute to the Jesuit Fathers. It is only when Cervantes comes to treat of the gypsies that he is treading unfamiliar ground, for, not having lived among them, he had no opportunity to study them at first hand and was dependent on hearsay. On the whole, however, the story is so close to the life of the age that it is possible to fix, approximately, the period in which the action occurs.

The "Colloquy" has been highly praised by critics, Professor Rudolph Schevill having described it as "one of the most precious documents that we possess for becoming acquainted in detail with Spanish culture and customs of the age in which Cervantes lived." The same authority goes on to observe:

Everything to Scipio [Cipión] and Berganza appears vile and despicable, and we cannot overlook the fine irony in the circumstance that it is dogs that hold this view of human life. . . . All in all, there is no denying that "The Colloquy of the Dogs" is a masterly portrait of manners, unexcelled in Spanish literature. Had there been no *Don Quixote*, this novel would still have provided an enduring base for Cervantes' fame as a great prose writer and incomparable painter of his fellowmen.

(Incidentally, it is possible that Nikolai Gogol was inspired by the "Colloquy" when, in his *Diary of a Madman* (*Zapiski sumashedshego*), he has two dogs engage in a discussion of human society.)

This *novela* has also a good deal to tell us about the author's aesthetic, social, and moral views. He gives us a criticism of the pastoral romance, an extremely unflattering picture of the theater of his day as he knew it, and a biting satire on pedants parading their Latin—though his own Latin was, to say the least, limited, as is shown by his misquotation of a passage from Horace, which he probably took from the Spanish version of Vicente Espinel (1591). He reaffirms his deep-seated aversion to satire as a form (a reflection of his innate geniality of temperament) even while indulging in it. His religious and moral views are, as usual, those of the good and enlightened Catholic, but in connection with his stern censure of the Moors one should recall the milder, more humane sentiments that he expresses in *Don Quixote*, Part II.

Significantly, it is once again on the theme of the dreamer and society—four dreamers in a charity ward—that the tale ends. In a sense it may be said that Cervantes from the beginning to the end of his career engaged in writing and rewriting his masterpiece, the immortal *Don Quixote*.

Three Exemplary Novels

Prologue: To the Reader

I should like, if it were possible, dearest reader, to be excused from writing this Prologue—the one I composed for my *Don Quixote* did not turn out so well for me that I should care to follow it here with another. In the present case, a certain friend of mine is to blame, one of the many whom I have acquired in the course of my life, thanks to my disposition rather than to my intellect. He might very well, as the custom is, have made an engraving of me for the frontispiece of this book; for the famous Don Juan de Jáuregui would have provided him with my portrait, and in that way my ambition would have been satisfied, as well as the desire that some have to know what kind of face and figure belong to him who has had the boldness to come out into the market place of the world and exhibit so many stories to the gaze of the peoples. Beneath the portrait my friend might have placed the following inscription:

"This man you see here with the aquiline countenance, the chestnut hair, the smooth, untroubled brow, the bright eyes, the hooked yet well proportioned nose, the silvery beard that less than a score of years ago was golden, the big mustache, the small mouth, the teeth that are scarcely worth mentioning (there are but half a dozen of them altogether, in bad condition and very badly placed, no two of them corresponding to another pair), the body of medium height, neither tall nor short, the high com-

plexion that is fair rather than dark, the slightly stooping shoulders, and the somewhat heavy build—this, I may tell you, is the
author of *La Galatea* and *Don Quixote de la Mancha;* [1] he it was
who composed the *Journey to Parnassus,* in imitation of Cesare
Caporali of Perusa, [2] as well as other works that are straying about
in these parts—without the owner's name, likely as not.

"He is commonly called Miguel de Cervantes Saavedra. He was
a soldier for many years and a captive for five and a half, an experience that taught him patience in adversity. In the naval battle
of Lepanto he lost his left hand as the result of a harquebus shot,
a wound which, however unsightly it may appear, he looks upon
as beautiful, for the reason that it was received on the most
memorable and sublime occasion that past ages have known or
those to come may hope to know; for he was fighting beneath
the victorious banner of the son of that thunderbolt of war,
Charles V of blessed memory."

And if this friend of mine of whom I am complaining had been
unable to think of anything else to say of me, I could have made
up and secretly given him a couple of dozen tributes to myself
such as would have spread my fame abroad and established my
reputation as a genius. For it is foolish to believe that such
eulogies are scrupulously truthful, since praise and blame never
have precise limits. But the short of it is the opportunity was
missed, and I have been left in the lurch and without a portrait.
Accordingly, I shall have to make use of my own tongue, which,
though a stammering one, will not falter when it comes to uttering truths that are understandable even when spoken in dumb
show.

And so, kind reader, I will further tell you that you will by no

---

[1] All references are to be found at the end of the book.

means be able to make a fricassee out of these *Novels* that I offer
you, for they have neither feet nor head nor entrails nor anything
that is suited to such a purpose; by which I mean to say that the
amorous episodes you will find in some of them are so respectable
and restrained, so within the bounds of reason and conformable
to Christian conduct, that no one who reads them, either carefully or carelessly, can possibly be moved to evil thoughts. I have
given these stories the title of Exemplary; and if you look closely
there is not one of them that does not afford a useful example.
If it were not that I do not wish to expand upon this subject, I
could show you the savory and wholesome fruit that is to be
had from each of them separately and from the collection as a
whole.

My intention has been to set up in the public square of our
country a billiard table where everyone may come to amuse himself without harm to body or soul; for decent and pleasing pastimes are profitable rather than harmful. One is not always in
church or engaged in prayer, one is not always occupied with
business matters, however important they may be. There is a
time for recreation, when the tired mind seeks repose. It is with
this object in view that public walks are laid out, water is brought
from afar to play in fountains, hills are leveled, and gardens culti-
vated with such care. There is one thing I will venture to say to
you: if I believed that the reading of these *Novels* would in any
way arouse an evil thought or desire, I would sooner cut off the
hand that wrote them than see them published. At my age one
does not trifle with the life to come—I am now sixty-four and a
little beyond.[3]

It is to this task that I devote my abilities, in accordance with my
natural inclination. What is more, I believe I am the first to have

written novels in the Castilian tongue, since the many that are printed in Spanish have all been translated from foreign languages, whereas these are my own, neither imitated nor stolen. My mind conceived them, my pen brought them forth, and they have grown in the arms of the printing press. Afterward, if I live long enough, I shall offer you the *Troubles of Persiles*, a book that dares to compete with Heliodorus (if only its boldness does not prove its undoing). But first you shall see, and shortly, the continuation of Don Quixote's exploits and Sancho Panza's drolleries, and after that, the *Garden Weeks*.

I am promising much in view of the little strength I have, but who can put a rein on ambition? I would merely ask you to bear in mind that inasmuch as I have had the audacity to dedicate these *Novels* to the great Count of Lemos, there must be some hidden virtue in them. I say no more, except: God be with you, and may He give me the patience to bear well the ill that a few stiff-starched hairsplitters are bound to speak of me. *Vale*.

RINCONETE
AND CORTADILLO

Rinconete and Cortadillo

At the Molinillo inn, which is situated on the border of the famous plains of Alcudia as one goes from Castile to Andalusia, two lads met by chance one hot summer day. They were around fourteen or fifteen years of age—neither, certainly, was more than sixteen—and both were good-looking enough though very ragged, tattered, and unkempt. Capes they had none, their trousers were of linen, their stockings of flesh. True, they had shoes, but those of the one boy were mere cord sandals that were just about worn out, while the other pair, of the "open work" variety, was minus soles and more nearly resembled fetters than anything else. One wore a green hunting cap, and his companion had on a low-crowned, broad-brimmed hat without a band. Over the latter's shoulder and wound about his chest was a chamois-colored beeswaxed shirt, caught up and stuffed into one sleeve.

The first youth, traveling light and without saddlebags, had what looked like a big lump on his bosom, which later turned out to be one of those Walloon ruffs, starched with grease and so well "embroidered" that it was nothing but a mass of threads. Wrapped up in this garment for safekeeping was a deck of cards, oval in shape, for the reason that, from long usage, the edges had been worn off, and in order that they might last longer they had been trimmed in this fashion. Both lads were sunburned, with long black-bordered nails and hands that were none too clean. One of them carried a short sword and the other a yellow-handled knife of the kind known as a cattle knife.

In the noontide heat, the two of them went out to a portico or lean-to that stood in front of the inn and, sitting down opposite each other, struck up a conversation.

"Sir Gentleman," said the older to the smaller boy, "what is your Grace's country and in what direction are you traveling?"

"Sir Cavalier," replied the one to whom the question had been put, "I do not know the name of my country, nor where I am bound."

"Well," said the older lad, "to be frank about it, you do not appear to be from Heaven, and since this is no place to be taking up your abode, you must be going farther."

"That I am," the younger one answered him. "But it was the truth I told you, for my land is not my land, seeing that all I have in it is a father who does not look upon me as a son and a step-mother who treats me the way one does a stepchild. I go where chance may take me until I find someone who will provide me with what I need to get through this wretched life of mine."

"And does your Grace know any trade?" inquired the big boy.

"None," said the small lad, "except how to run like a hare, leap like a deer, and handle a pair of scissors very neatly."

"All that," the other one assured him, "is very good and useful

and a great advantage; for your Grace is bound to find some sacristan who will give you the offering for All Saints if you will cut him some paper flowers for the Tomb that they erect on the altar on Holy Thursday."

"That is not the kind of cutting I do," replied the younger one. "My father, by the grace of Heaven, is a tailor and hose maker, and he taught me to cut leggings, which, as your Grace very well knows, are half-hose with gaiters, properly called spatter-dashes. I cut them so well, really, that I could pass my examination as a master of the craft. The only thing is, my luck is cut so short that my talents go unrecognized."

"All that and more," said the big boy, "happens to the capable. I have always heard it said that the finest talents are the most unappreciated; but your Grace is young and you still have time to mend your luck. If I am not mistaken and my eyes do not deceive me, you have other accomplishments, which you prefer to keep secret."

"That I have," the small boy admitted, "but they are not for the public gaze, as your Grace has very well remarked."

"In that case," said the other lad, "I may tell you that I am one of the most tight-lipped young fellows that you will find for many a mile around here; and in order that your Grace may feel free to unbosom yourself and confide in me, I will first tell you all about my own life, for I think it is not without some hidden purpose that fate has brought us together, and I believe that from now on to our dying day we are going to be true friends.

"I, noble sir," he went on, "am a native of Fuenfrida, a village well known and even famous on account of the distinguished travelers who are constantly passing through it. My name is Pedro del Rincón,[1] and my father is a person of quality, being an

agent of the Holy Crusade, that is to say, one who sells papal bulls
or indulgences, a *bulero*, or, as people usually say, a *buldero*. I
used to accompany him at times, and I learned the trade so well
that when it comes to dispensing bulls, I would not take second
place to any man no matter how good at it he might be. But one
day I came to love the money from the bulls more than the bulls
themselves, and having embraced a bag of it, I made off for Madrid, where, with the facilities which that city commonly affords,
I gutted the bag in a very short while and left it with more creases
than a bridegroom's handkerchief.

"The one who was in charge of the money then came after me,
I was arrested, and they showed me little mercy; although, when
those gentlemen saw how young I was, they were satisfied with
sending me to the whipping post and swatting the flies off my back
for a spell, after which I was forbidden to set foot in the capital
for a period of four years. But I was patient; I merely shrugged
my shoulders and put up with the flogging and the swatting, and
was in such a hurry to begin serving my sentence of exile that I
did not even have time to get me any sumpter mules. I took what
I could of my valuables, those that I thought I was most likely to
need, including these cards." (With this, he displayed the deck
we have mentioned, which he carried in his Walloon ruff.) "With
them I have earned my living by playing twenty-one in all the
inns and taverns between here and Madrid. They are, as you can
see, worn and filthy, but there is one marvelous thing about them
for him who knows how to handle them, and that is the fact that
no matter how you cut them, you are bound to turn up an ace.

"If your Grace is at all acquainted with this game, you can see
what an advantage a player has who is certain of an ace the first
card he cuts, for it will count either one point or eleven, and with

the stakes set at twenty-one, his money will stay at home. In addition, I learned from a cook in the household of a certain ambassador a number of tricks at lansquenet and the game known as *andaboba;* so that, if your Grace is able to pass his examination as a cutter of leggings, I could be a master of the science that Vilhan invented.[2] That way, I am sure not to die of hunger; for in any farmhouse to which I come there is someone who is willing to pass the time with a little game, as we are going to find very shortly. Let us spread the net and see if any bird falls into it from among the mule drivers in this inn; by which I mean that the two of us will start playing twenty-one as if we were in earnest, and if anyone wants to make a third, he will be the first to leave his money behind him."

"That suits me," said the other lad. "I thank your Grace very much for giving me an account of your life, and I feel that I must now tell you my own life story, which very briefly is as follows. I was born in the pious village that lies between Salamanca and Medina del Campo. My father is a tailor and taught me his trade; and with my ability, from cutting with shears I went on to cutting purses. I became tired of the cramped life in a small town and the lack of affection my stepmother showed me, and so I left and went to Toledo to practice my calling there. In that city I did wonders; for there was not a reliquary dangling from a hood or a pocket so well hidden that my fingers did not find it out or my scissors clip it, even though it might have been guarded by the eyes of Argus.

"During the four months I spent in Toledo I never once was trapped between doors or caught in the act or chased by constables or turned up by any informer. True enough, there was one week when a spy who worked both with the officers of the law and with us reported my cleverness to the magistrate, who became so enamored of my good qualities that he insisted on seeing me. However, being very humble, I do not like to deal with important personages, and I avoided him by leaving the city in such haste that I too did not have time to provide myself with sumpter mules or small change or a post-chaise or even so much as a cart."

"Never mind about that," said Rincón. "Since we know one another now, there is no need for all these grand airs. Let us make a clean breast of it and admit that we haven't a penny between us or even a pair of shoes."

"So be it," replied Diego Cortado (for that was the younger one's name),[3] "and since our friendship, as you have said, Señor Rincón, is to be lifelong, let us begin with the time-honored ceremonies."

Saying this, Cortado arose, and he and Rincón clasped each other in a warm embrace, then started playing twenty-one with the aforementioned cards, which may have been clean of dust and straw (that is to say, of the king's dues), but not of grease and trickery. After a few hands Diego was able to cut an ace quite as well as his teacher, and when a mule driver came out to the portico for an airing and asked if he could make a third, they agreed readily enough and in less than half an hour had won twelve reales and twenty-two maravedis, which for the muleteer was equivalent to a dozen stabs in the back and twenty-two thousand sorrows. Thinking that, being mere lads, they would not be able to prevent him from doing so, he tried to take the money away from them; but one of the boys drew his short sword and the other his yellow-handled knife and gave him so much trouble that, if his companions had not run out, things undoubtedly would have gone hard with him.

At this point, a group of travelers on horseback happened to come along the road. They were on the way to take their siesta at the Alcalde inn half a league beyond; but seeing the fight between the mule driver and the lads, they hastened to separate them, telling the latter that in case they were bound for Seville, they might join the party.

"That is where we are going," said Rincón, "and we will serve your Lordships and obey your every command."

Without any further hesitation the pair leaped out into the road in front of the mules and took their departure, leaving their victim despoiled of his cash and very angry, while the innkeeper's wife marveled at the good training the rogues had had, for she had been eavesdropping on their conversation. When she told the muleteer that she had heard them say the cards were false ones, he began tearing at his beard and wanted to follow them to the other hostelry in order to get his money back; for, as he said, it was a very great insult, touching upon a point of honor, that two boys should have been able to trick a grown man like him. His companions, however, restrained him, advising him that he should not advertise his lack of cleverness and his gullibility. The short of it is that, while they did not succeed in consoling him, by dint of much talking they prevailed upon him to stay where he was.

In the meantime Cortado and Rincón proved to be such zealous servants that the travelers gave them a lift most of the way, and although they had a number of opportunities to rifle the luggage of their temporary masters they did not do so, since they did not wish to lose so good a chance for making the journey to Seville, a town they very much wished to see. Nevertheless, as they entered the city—which they did at the vesper hour and by the Customhouse Gate in order that the baggage might be inspected and the duty paid—Cortado could not refrain from ripping open the valise or satchel that one of the company, a Frenchman, carried up behind him on the crupper of his mount. With his knife he inflicted so wide and deep a gash that the insides were plainly visible, and he then slyly took out a couple of good shirts, a sun dial, and a small memorandum book.

The lads were none too well pleased at seeing these objects, and assuming that inasmuch as the Frenchman kept the satchel with him it must contain something of greater worth than what they had found in it, they were tempted to make another search but did not do so, thinking that by this time the owner would have removed and put away for safekeeping whatever was left. And so, before the theft had been discovered, they took their leave of those who had been their providers up to now, and the next day they sold the shirts at the old clothes market outside the Arenal Gate, receiving for them the sum of twenty reales.

Having done this, they set out to see the town. They marveled at the size and magnificence of the cathedral and the great throng of people on the river bank; for this was the season for provisioning the fleet, and there were six galleys drawn up along the wharf, the sight of which caused the youths to heave a sigh and fear the day when their misdeeds would take them to the rowing benches for the rest of their lives. They also gazed at the many porters with baskets who were going up and down, and they asked one of them how he liked his job, if there was much work to it, and how much he made. It was a young Asturian whom they questioned, and he replied that it was a very good job on the whole, with no tax to pay, adding that some days he made as much as five or six reales, with which he could eat and drink and have a

royal good time, being free to seek whatever employer he liked
without having to put up any security, and he was sure, also, of
having his dinner whenever he wished, as meals were served at all
hours even in the meanest chophouse.

The two friends thought that this did not sound at all bad, and
the work was not displeasing to them. Indeed, it seemed to them
admirably suited to the practice of their own trade under cover
and in safety, for as porters they would find it easy to enter private houses everywhere. They accordingly decided to buy the
necessary equipment, seeing there was no examination to be
passed, and they asked the Asturian what they should purchase.
He told them they needed a couple of small bags, new or at any
rate clean, and that each of them should have three palm-fiber
baskets, two large ones and a small one, to carry the meat, fish,
and fruit—the bags were for the bread.

He then took them where these articles were for sale, and they,
with the money they had got for the Frenchman's shirts, bought
all the articles in question. Within a couple of hours they had become quite expert at their new trade, as could be seen from the
manner in which they handled their baskets and carried their
bags; and their mentor thereupon proceeded to inform them
where it was they should put in an appearance: mornings at the
Meat Market and in San Salvador Square; on fish days at the Fish
Market and the Slope; every afternoon at the river; and on Thurs-
days at the Fair.

This lesson they memorized thoroughly, and early the next
morning they took up their stand in the Square. No sooner had
they arrived than they were surrounded by other youths engaged
in the same occupation, who, seeing the spick-and-span condition of their bags and baskets, judged them to be newcomers.

They had to answer innumerable questions and did so very cautiously. Meanwhile, a young student and a soldier had come up, and, observing what clean baskets the novices had, the former summoned Cortado while the latter took Rincón.

"In the name of God, so be it!" both lads cried.[4]

"Sir," said Rincón, "this is a good way to begin, with my first tip coming from your Grace."

"The tip," said the soldier, "will not be a bad one; for I have won a little money and I am in love, and I am giving a banquet today for some of my lady's women friends."

"Very well then, your Grace, go ahead and load me down as much as you like, for I have the will and the strength to carry away this entire market place, and if necessary I'll be glad to help you cook the food as well."

The soldier was pleased with the boy's good manners and told him that if he wished to become a servant he would take him out of such degrading employment; to which Rincón replied that, since this was his first day, he would like to see how good or bad a calling it was, but in case he was not satisfied with it, he promised on his word that he would enter the soldier's service before he would that of a canon. The soldier gave a laugh and loaded the boy well, then pointed out the house where his lady dwelt so that Rincón would know it from then on and he would not have to accompany him when he sent him on an errand. The lad promised to be loyal and well behaved, and the man then gave him three cuartos, and in no time at all Rincón was back at the Square so that he might not miss any chance that offered; for the Asturian had warned him that he must keep a sharp eye out, and had further advised him that, when he was carrying small fish such as dace, sardines, or flounders, he might very well take a few and eat them himself, if only to help defray the expenses of the day; but he reminded him that it should be done with a great deal of caution so that he would not lose his good reputation, which was the most important thing in this business.

Although Rincón had returned as quickly as he could, he found Cortado already back at his post, and his companion now came up and asked how things had gone with him. Rincón opened his hand and displayed the three cuartos, whereupon Cortado brought out from his bosom a purse that once upon a time had been of amber-scented leather and appeared to be rather well filled.

"It was with this," he said, "and a couple of cuartos that his reverence the student paid me off; but take it, Rincón, for fear of what may happen."

He had barely slipped the purse to him when the student came running up in a sweat and frightened to death. Seeing Cortado, he asked if by any chance the boy had seen a purse answering such and such a description and containing fifteen gold crowns, three pieces of two reales each, and a number of cuartos and ochavos, amounting to a certain sum in maravedis. He demanded to know if the porter had taken his money while he, the student, was making his purchases.

Cortado answered with great craftiness and without the slightest sign of agitation. "All that I can tell you about that purse," he said, "is that it surely could not have been lost unless you were careless about where you put it."

"Sinner that I am!" exclaimed the student. "I must have been careless, seeing that they stole it from me."

"That is what I say," Cortado agreed; "but there is a remedy for everything in this world except death, and the first and chief remedy that your Grace should try is patience, remembering that God made us all, and one day follows another, and things come and go. It may be that, in the course of time, the one who took the purse will repent and return it to your Grace nicely perfumed."

"We'll forget about the perfume," said the student.

"And then," Cortado went on, "there are letters of excommunication and interdicts, and there is also such a thing as diligence, which is the mother of good fortune. But to tell you the truth, I shouldn't like to have that purse on me, for if your Grace has any holy orders, I would feel as if I had committed some great incest or sacrilege."

"Sacrilege indeed!" cried the grief-stricken student. "Although I am not a priest but merely a sacristan to a few nuns, the money in that purse was the third part of the revenue from a chaplaincy which a priest who is a friend of mine sent me to collect, and so it is money that is holy and sacred."

"Let him eat it with his bread," said Rincón at this point. "I wouldn't go his security for all he will get from it. There is a day of judgment when everything will come out in the wash, and then we shall see who the scoundrel was who dared to take, steal, and make away with a third of the income from a chapel."

"Tell me, Sir Sacristan, upon your life, how much does the income amount to each year?"

"Income! I'm a son of a whore!" The sacristan was beside himself with anger. "Am I to stand here and discuss the income with you? If you know anything, brothers, tell me; if not, be on your way and Godspeed, for I must go and have the crier announce it."

"That is not a bad idea," said Cortado. "But your Grace must be sure not to forget the description of the purse or the exact amount of money that was in it, for if you are off as much as a

penny you will never see it again as long as you live, and that is a prophecy." [5]

"There is nothing to fear on that score," replied the sacristan, "for I remember it all better than I do the sound of the bells I ring. I shall not err by the fraction of a point."

With this, he took from his pocket a lace-bordered handkerchief to wipe the sweat that was dripping from his face as from a still, and no sooner did Cortado lay eyes upon it than he marked it for his own. As the sacristan went away Cortado followed and overtook him on the cathedral stairs, where he called him to one side and began spouting such an interminable rigmarole of nonsense having to do with the theft of the purse and the hope of its recovery that the poor student was quite bewildered as he listened. Unable to understand what the youth was saying, the sacristan had him repeat it two or three times; and thus they stood there, staring each other straight in the eye, with the sacristan hanging on every word and so bewildered that Cortado found the opportunity for which he was waiting and slyly took the handkerchief from its owner's pocket. Then he said good-by, promising to see him again that afternoon. He had his eyes, he said, on another porter, a lad of about the same build, who was something of a thief and whom he suspected of having stolen the purse; he would make it his business to find out within a day or two.

Somewhat consoled by this, the sacristan took his leave, and the boy then joined Rincón, who had been looking on from a distance. Not far away there was another lad with a basket who had witnessed everything that had taken place and who had seen Cortado give the handkerchief to Rincón. He now approached them.

"Tell me, gallant sirs," he said, "are you in the bad books or not?"

"Gallant sir," Rincón answered him, "we do not understand that kind of talk."

"What! You mean to say you are not, gentle Murcians?" [6]

"We are neither from Thebes [7] nor from Murcia," said Cortado. "If there is anything else that you want to know, speak out. If not, go your way, and may God go with you."

"So you do not understand?" said the young man. "Very well then, I will feed it to you with a silver spoon. What I meant to inquire, gentlemen, was whether or not you are thieves, though I do not know why I should ask, since I can see that you are. But tell me, how does it come that you have not yet gone to Señor Monipodio's customhouse?" [8]

"Why, Sir Gallant," said Rincón, "can it be that thieves in this country have to pay a duty?"

"If they do not pay," the other lad replied, "they at least have to register with Señor Monipodio, who is their father, their teacher, and their protector; and I accordingly advise you to come with me and render him obedience, for if you do not do so and dare to commit a theft without his approval, it will cost you dearly."

"I thought," remarked Cortado, "that thieving was a trade that was free of tax or duty, and that if you paid, it was in a lump sum with your neck or your shoulders as security. But since that is the way it is and each land has its own customs, let us observe those of this country, which, being the leading one in all the world, must have the best usages. Accordingly, your Grace may show us where this gentleman you speak of is to be found, for I suspect from what I have heard of him that he is a very influential personage, big-hearted, and a very clever hand at the business."

"Indeed he is influential, clever, and competent!" was the youth's rejoinder; "so much so that during the four years that he has been our leader and our father, not more than four of us have ended up on the *finibusterrae*, only some thirty have tasted leather, and a mere sixty-two have gone over the road." [9]

"Sir," said Rincón, "the truth is, we come as near to understanding you as we do to flying."

"Let us start walking, and I will explain these terms on the way, together with others that ought to be as familiar to you as the bread in your mouth." He then went on to give them the meaning of various expressions drawn from that form of speech that is known as *germanía*, or thieves' slang. His discourse was not a short one, for they had a long way to go.

"Is your Grace by any chance a thief?" Rincón inquired of their guide.

"Yes," he answered, "that I am, and at the service of God and all good people; although I am not one of the best, seeing that I am still in the first year of my apprenticeship."

"That is something new to me," said Cortado, "to hear that thieves are in this world to serve God and good people."

"Sir," replied the youth, "I do not meddle with tologies; [10] all I know is that everyone in this business may praise God, especially in view of the order that Monipodio keeps among his adopted sons."

"Undoubtedly," observed Rincón, "his rule must be a good and holy one if he is able to make thieves serve God."

"It is so good and holy that I do not know if it could be improved in any way, so far as our trade is concerned. He has commanded that out of what we steal we must give something in the way of alms to buy oil for the lamp that stands before a highly venerated image here in this city; and I must say that this act of piety has had great results, for only recently they gave the *ansia* three times to a *cuatrero* who had done a Murcian on a couple of *roznos*, and though he was weak from quartan fever, he endured it all without singing, as if it were nothing at all, and we who are in the business attributed this to his devoutness, for such strength as he had was not of itself sufficient to enable him to stand the executioner's first *desconcierto*.

"And since I know that you are going to ask me what some of these words mean, I shall cure myself while I am healthy and tell you before you put the question. You may know, then, that a *cuatrero* is a cattle thief; *ansia* is the torture; *roznos* are asses, begging your pardon; and the first *desconcierto* is the turn of the screw that the executioner gives at the start. We do more than that, however: we say our rosary, which is divided according to days of the week, and many of us do not steal on Friday or speak to any woman called Mary on a Saturday."

"All of that sounds marvelous to me," said Cortado; "but tell me, your Grace, do you make any other form of restitution or do any other kind of penance?"

"As for restitution," the youth explained, "there is no use talking about that since it is out of the question on account of the many portions into which the loot is divided, with each of the agents and contracting parties [11] getting his share. For that reason, the one who commits the theft cannot restore anything, and so far as that is concerned, there is no one to urge us to do so. We never go to confession, and if letters of excommunication are issued against us, we never hear of them as we are not in church when they are read, unless it happens to be a feast day and we are attracted there by what is to be had from the great crowd of people."

"And by doing merely this," said Cortado, "you gentlemen think that your life is good and holy, do you?"

"Why, what is there bad about it?" the young man asked. "Isn't it worse to be a heretic or a renegade, to kill your father and mother, or to be a solomite?"

"Your Grace means a sodomite," said Rincón.

"That is what I said."

"It is all bad," said Cortado, "but seeing that our fate would have us enter this brotherhood, let your Grace lead on. I am dying to see this Señor Monipodio, having heard so many fine things about him."

"You will soon have your wish," said the youth, "for there is his house. You gentlemen may wait at the door while I go in to find out if he is free, this being the hour at which he commonly grants an audience.

"Very well," said Rincón.

When they had gone on a little farther the young fellow entered a house that was not very good, indeed it was quite unprepossessing, and the other two waited for him at the door. Soon afterward he came out and called to them, and they entered, their guide telling them to wait a while longer in a small brick-paved courtyard so clean and well scrubbed that it appeared to be covered with the finest carmine. On one side was a three-legged stool and on the other a pitcher with a broken spout on top of which stood a small jug that was in equally bad shape. On the third side was a reed mat and in the middle of it a flower pot, or, as they are called in Seville, a sweet basil jar.

As they waited for Señor Monipodio to come down, the two

lads attentively eyed the furnishings of the house, and as he delayed putting in an appearance, Rincón ventured into one of two low rooms that opened upon the patio. In it he saw two fencing foils and a couple of cork shields suspended from the wall by four nails, a large chest without a lid or covering of any sort, and three other reed mats spread out on the ground. On the wall opposite him was one of those cheap prints of Our Lady, and beneath it was suspended a palm-fiber basket with a white vessel nearby set into the wall, from which Rincón gathered that the basket served as a poor box while the vessel was for holy water, and this turned out to be the truth.

At that moment two youths, each about twenty years old, came in. They were dressed like students and were followed shortly afterward by two porters and a blind man; without saying a word, they all began strolling up and down the courtyard. It was not long before two old men entered, baize-clad and wearing spectacles, which gave them a grave and dignified appearance, as did the rosaries with tinkling beads that they carried in their hands. Behind them came an old woman in a full skirt. She was as silent as the others; she went into the room off the side, took some holy water, and very devoutly knelt before the image. She remained there for some little while; then, having first kissed the ground and lifted her arms and eyes heavenward three times in succession, she arose, tossed some coins into the basket, and came out to join the others in the patio.

In short, before many minutes had elapsed, there were upwards of fourteen persons assembled there, variously clad and from different walks in life. Among the latest arrivals were a couple of swaggering young ruffians with large mustaches, broad-brimmed hats, Walloon ruffs, colored stockings, and large showy garters. Their swords exceeded the length allowed by law, each carried a brace of pistols in place of daggers, and their bucklers were suspended from their girdles. Upon entering, they glanced at Rincón and Cortado out of the corner of their eyes, as if surprised at seeing strangers there, and, going up to them, inquired if they were members of the brotherhood. Rincón replied that they were, and were at the service of their Graces.

Then it was that Señor Monipodio came down, and all of that respectable company were very glad to see him. He appeared to be around forty-five or forty-six years of age, and was a tall man with a dark complexion, close-set brows, and a heavy black beard; his eyes were deep in his head. He had on a shirt without a doublet, and through the opening at his throat could be seen what looked like a forest, so hairy-chested was he. He wore a cloak of baize that fell almost to his feet, which were shod in a pair of old shoes made into slippers. His legs were covered down to the ankles with wide linen breeches, and his hat, with bell-shaped crown and a broad brim, was the kind worn by wandering rogues. From a shoulder belt strapped across his bosom there hung a broadsword resembling those of the "Little Dog" brand.[12] He had short hairy hands and fat fingers with blunted nails. Nothing could be seen of his legs, but his feet were monstrosities, for they were sprawling and covered with bunions. The short of it is, he was the coarsest and most hideous barbarian in all the world. He was accompanied by the one who had brought the two boys there. Their guide, taking them by the hand, now presented them.

"These, Señor Monipodio," he said, "are the good lads I was telling you about. Let your Grace examine them and see whether or not they are worthy of entering our fraternity."

"That I will very gladly do," replied Monipodio.

I have neglected to state that as Monipodio came in all those who were waiting for him immediately dropped him a profound and sweeping curtsy, with the exception of the two ruffians, who merely lifted their hats in a don't-give-a-damn manner (as their kind are in the habit of saying) and then resumed their stroll along one side of the courtyard as he walked up and down the other side. Turning to the newcomers, Monipodio inquired concerning their profession, the country from which they came, and their parentage. It was Rincón who answered him.

"Our profession speaks for itself, seeing that we are here in your Grace's presence. Our country does not seem to me to be of any great importance, nor our parents either, since it is not a question of giving information prior to being received into some respectable order."

"You are quite right about that, my son," said Monipodio. "It is a good idea to conceal the things you speak of; for if luck does not turn out as it should, it is not desirable to have some such entry as this in the books of justice beneath the court clerk's seal: 'So-and-So, son of So-and-So, native of such and such a place, on such and such a day, was hanged or flogged,' or something of that sort, which to say the least does not sound well in the ears of God-fearing folk. And so, I repeat, there is an advantage in concealing your place of origin and your parentage, and even in changing your names, although among ourselves nothing is to be kept secret. For the present, your own names will be enough."

Rincón and Cortado then gave him the information he desired.

"From now on," continued Monipodio, "it is my will that you, Rincón, should be known as Rinconete, and you, Cortado, as Cortadillo, these being names that are very well suited to your age and the rules of our order. In accordance with those rules,

however, it is also necessary for us to know the parents' names, for it is our custom every year to have certain masses said for the souls of deceased relatives and for our benefactors. We set apart a certain portion of the swag to pay the fee of the officiating priest; and it is said that these masses, thus duly sung and paid for, are of great benefit to such poor souls, by way of shipwreck.[13]

"Under the heading of our benefactors we include the one who defends us in court; the constable who tips us off; the executioner who shows us mercy; and the person who, when one of our number is fleeing through the street and the crowd in full cry behind him is crying 'Stop thief! Stop thief!' intervenes to stem the torrent of pursuers by saying, 'Let the poor fellow go, he's had enough bad luck, let him go, and let his sin be his punishment!' Then there are those feminine benefactors who with their sweat aid us in prison and in the galleys alike. There are the fathers and mothers who brought us into the world; and there is the court clerk who, if things go as they should, sees to it that there is no crime that is not a misdemeanor and no misdemeanor that gets much punishment. Our brotherhood observes the adversery of each one of these every year with all the pomposity and solemnitude in our power."

"Surely," said Rinconete (who had now been confirmed with this name), "all that is worthy of the most lofty and profound genius which we have heard that you, Señor Monipodio, possess. Our parents are still living, but if they should pass away, we will at once notify this most blessed and well-protected confraternity in order that their shipwreck or storm,[14] the adversery that your Grace speaks of, may be celebrated with the usual solemnity and pomp, unless you think it could be done better with pomposity and solemnitude as your Grace has just remarked."

"That is the way it shall be done," declared Monipodio, "or there will not be so much as a piece left of me." And, calling to the guide, he said, "Come here, Ganchuelo.[15] Have the sentries been posted?"

"Yes," replied the guide (whose name was Ganchuelo), "there are three of them on watch, and there is no reason for us to fear being taken by surprise."

"Coming back, then, to what we were talking about," Monipodio went on, "I would like to know, my sons, what it is you can do, so that I can give you work of the kind you like and suited to your abilities."

"I," answered Rinconete, "know a little trick or two with the pasteboards; I can play them from up my sleeve or under the table; I've a sharp eye for a smudged card or one that's been scraped; I'm a good hand at ombre, four-spot, and eight-spot; I don't take second place to anyone when it comes to shuffling or dealing from the bottom of the deck. As for light-fingered work, I'm right at home there, there's no one to equal me as third man in a confidence game, and I can stack 'em against the best there are." [16]

"That's all right for a start," said Monipodio, "but it's all old stuff that any beginner knows, and is only good when you get a sucker in the small hours of the morning. But time will tell and we shall see. With this foundation and half a dozen lessons, I trust to God that I shall be able to make of you a famous workman and possibly even a master craftsman."

"We will do anything we can to serve your Grace and the other gentlemen of the confraternity," said Rinconete.

"And you, Cortadillo, what are your accomplishments?" Monipodio asked.

"I," replied Cortadillo, "know the trick that is called 'put in two and take out five.' [17] I can pick a pocket with neatness and dispatch."

"Anything else?" Monipodio wanted to know.

"No," said Cortadillo, "I'm very sorry, but there isn't."

"Don't let it worry you, my son," said Monipodio, "for you've reached a safe harbor where you will not drown, and a school where you will learn, before you leave, all that you most need to know. But what about the matter of nerve, my lads, how goes it on that score?"

"How should it go with us," said Rinconete, "except very well? We have nerve enough for any undertaking that our profession calls for."

"That is good," said Monipodio, "but what I want to know is, do you have enough to stand it if they give you the *ansia* half a dozen times and not open your lips or call your mouth your own?"

"We already know what *ansia* means, Señor Monipodio," Cortadillo told him, "and we are ready for anything; for we are not so ignorant as to fail to realize that what the tongue says the throat must pay for. We know that Heaven shows plenty of mercy to the bold man (to give him no other name) who, with life and death depending on what he says, acts as if there were more letters in a *no* than in a *si*."

"That will do," said Monipodio at this point. "There is no need of your saying anything more. I may tell you that this one conversation that I have had with you has convinced, obliged, persuaded, and compelled me to give you from now on the rank of senior members, and dispense with the customary one year's apprenticeship."

"I am of the same opinion," declared one of the ruffians. And

all those present approved the decision, for they had been listening to everything that was said, and they now asked Monipodio
to grant the two lads permission to enjoy all the immunities of
the brotherhood, by reason of the good impression the pair had
made and their way of talking, which showed that they fully
deserved the favor. He replied that he would grant the request
by bestowing upon the youths, from now on, the prerogatives
mentioned, and at the same time he reminded Rinconete and Cortadillo that they should value all this very highly since it meant
they would not have to pay the usual tax of one-half of the
first theft they committed or perform any menial functions
throughout the whole of the first year; they would not have to
carry messages from his agents to any senior brother whether in
jail or at the house; [18] they might take their wine straight and eat
when and where they liked without asking permission of their
leader, and henceforth they would share as fully fledged members
in whatever the older ones brought in.

These and other advantages that were offered them the two lads
looked upon as a most exceptional favor and they were very polite
in expressing their thanks to Señor Monipodio.

At that moment a lad came running up all out of breath. "The
constable in charge of vagabonds," he announced, "is coming
to this house, but he does not have his men with him."

"Let no one get excited," Monipodio directed. "He is a friend
and never comes to do us harm; so calm yourselves, and I will go
out and have a word with him."

With this, they all quieted down, for they had been somewhat
alarmed. Monipodio, meanwhile, went out the door and stood for
some time talking to the constable, then returned and asked, "Who
was stationed in San Salvador Square today?"

"I was," said the one who had acted as guide.

"Well then," Monipodio demanded, "how does it come that you did not report an amber purse which someone made away with in that neighborhood, containing fifteen gold crowns, two double reales, and I can't tell you how many cuartos?"

"It is true," admitted the guide, "that such a purse was missing today, but I did not take it, nor do I have any idea who did."

"Don't be playing any tricks with me," Monipodio warned. "That purse must be produced, for the constable who is asking about it is a friend and does us countless good turns every year."

The youth again swore that he knew nothing about it, whereupon Monipodio became so angry that his eyes darted sparks.

"Let no one," he said, "think to jest by breaking the slightest rule of our order, for if he does it will cost him his life. That purse has to be produced. If it is being concealed to avoid payment of the tax, I myself will put up whatever is necessary out of my own pocket, for the constable must by all means be satisfied."

Ganchuelo once more began swearing, with many oaths and curses, that he had not taken the purse nor so much as laid eyes on it; all of which merely added fuel to Monipodio's wrath and caused a stir of excitement among all the others present at seeing their statutes and worthy ordinances thus broken. In view of all this dissension and agitation, Rinconete thought it would be a good thing to calm them down and at the same time please his superior, who was bursting with indignation; and so, having consulted with his friend Cortadillo, and with the latter's consent, he brought out the sacristan's purse.

"Let there be no further question about this matter, gentlemen," he said. "Here is the purse, and in it you will find all that the constable said it contained. My comrade Cortadillo lifted it today, along with a handkerchief which he took from the same person."

Cortadillo then brought out the handkerchief and displayed it. Upon sight of it, Monipodio said, "Cortadillo *the Good*, for such is the name and title by which he is to be known from now on, may keep this kerchief, which may be charged to my account. But as for the purse, it must go back to the constable, who is a relative of the sacristan's. We must comply with the old proverb which says: 'To one who has given you a whole chicken, you can spare a drumstick.' This worthy officer does more for us in a day than we could do for him in a hundred days."

By common consent, those present approved the gentlemanlike conduct of the newcomers and the decision of their superior, who now went out to return the purse to the constable, while Cortadillo was left with a new name, that of *the Good*, just as if he had been Don Alonso Pérez de Guzmán *the Good*, the one who from the walls of Tarifa threw down the knife with which his only child was beheaded.[19]

When Monipodio returned he was accompanied by two girls with painted faces, rouged lips, and bosoms whitened with ceruse. They wore serge half-mantles [20] and were so carefree and shameless in their demeanor that Rinconete and Cortadillo at once recognized them as coming from the brothel, an assumption that was perfectly correct. As soon as they entered they threw open their arms, and one ran up to Chiquiznaque, the other to Maniferro, for these were the names of the two ruffians, Maniferro's being due to the fact that he had an iron hand in place of the one that had been cut off as a punishment for his crimes. The pair embraced the newcomers joyfully and asked if they had brought anything to wet the gullet.[21]

"How could we fail you, my swordsman?" replied the one who was called Gananciosa.[22] "Your runner Silbatillo will be here shortly with a clothesbasket filled with what God has been pleased to give us."

This proved to be the truth, for at that very instant a lad came in bearing a hamper covered with a sheet. They were all very glad to see Silbato, and Monipodio at once ordered them to bring one of the reed mats from the little room off the side and spread it out in the middle of the patio. He then commanded them all to sit down around it in order that they might have a little snack and talk business at the same time. At this point, the old woman who had been praying in front of the image spoke up.

"Monipodio, my son," she said, "I am in no mood for feasting today. For a couple of days now I have had a dizziness in the head that drives me mad, and what's more, I must go finish my devotions before noon and place my candles in front of Our Lady of the Waters and the Holy Crucifix of Saint Augustine, something that I would not fail to do come snow or blizzard. What happened was this. Last night the Renegade and the Centipede brought to my house a washbasket somewhat larger than this one and filled with white linen. I swear to God and upon my soul, the clothes were still wet and covered with suds, which the poor fellows had not had time to remove; and they were sweating so much beneath the weight of the hamper that it was a pity to see the water dripping and pouring from their faces—they were so red that it gave them the appearance of a couple of cherubs.

"They told me that they were on the trail of a cattle dealer who had just weighed in a flock of lambs at the slaughterhouse, as they wished to get their fingers into a big catskin bag filled with reales that he carried on his person. They did not take the linen out to count it but trusted entirely to my conscience; and may God fulfill my worthy desires and free us all from the clutches of the law, I did not touch the basket, and you will find everything just as it was."

"I believe everything you say, mother," said Monipodio. "Let it stay where it is, and at nightfall I will come and make an inventory of what it contains and will give each one exactly what is coming to him, as I always do."

"Let it be as you have commanded, my son," said the old woman, "and since it is getting late, give me a little swig, if you have one, to comfort this stomach of mine which is feeling very faint."

"Indeed you shall have a drink, mother!" said Escalanta,[23] for that was the name of Gananciosa's companion. She uncovered the basket and brought out a leather flask with nearly two arrobas of wine and a cork vessel that with no trouble at all would hold an azumbre.[24] After filling the vessel, Escalanta gave it to the devout old woman, who took it in both her hands.

"You have poured me a lot, daughter Escalanta," she said, blowing off a little of the foam, "but God will give me strength for everything." And putting her lips to the brim, she drank it all down at a single gulp without pausing for breath. "That's from Guadalcanal," she remarked, "and it has a wee taste of gypsum.[25] May God comfort you, my daughter, who have thus comforted me. The only thing I am afraid of is that it may do me harm, for I have had nothing to eat."

"It won't hurt you, mother," said Monipodio, "for it's over three years old."

"In the Virgin's name, I hope you're right," the old woman

answered, and she went on, "Look, my daughters, and see if by any chance you have a spare cuarto to pay for my candles. Being anxious to bring you news of the basket, I came away in such a hurry that I left my purse at home."

"Yes, I have something for you, Señora Pipota," replied Gananciosa (Pipota was the old woman's name).[26] "Here are two cuartos for you, and with one of them I wish you would buy a candle for me and place it in front of Señor Saint Michael; and if you have enough for two, offer the other to Señor Saint Blas, for they are my patron saints. I'd like to have you place one before the image of Señora Saint Lucy also, as I am devoted to her for the sake of the eyes;[27] but I have no more small change, so that will have to wait for another day when I can pay my respects to all of them."

"You will be very wise in doing so, daughter. See to it that you are not miserly; for it is very important to carry your own candles before you die and not wait for your heirs or executors to do it for you."

"Mother Pipota is quite right about that," said Escalanta, putting her hand into her purse. She gave the old woman another cuarto, directing her to place two more candles before whatever saints she thought would be most appreciative and helpful.

"Enjoy yourselves, children," said Pipota as she prepared to leave. "Enjoy yourselves now while there is time, for when old age comes you will weep as I do for all the moments you lost in youth. Remember me to God in your prayers. I go to pray for myself and you, that He may free and preserve us in this dangerous trade of ours, and keep us out of the hands of the law."

With this she went away. When she had left they all sat down around the mat and Gananciosa spread the sheet for a tablecloth.

The first thing she brought out of the hamper was a large bunch of radishes and some two dozen oranges and lemons, followed by a large earthenware pot filled with slices of fried codfish. There was also half a Dutch cheese, a jug of fine olives, a platter of shrimp, and a great quantity of crabs, with a thirst-inspirer in the form of capers drowned in peppers, together with three very white loaves of Gandul bread.[28]

There were around fourteen at the meal, and none of them failed to bring out his yellow-handled knife, with the exception of Rinconete, who made use of his short sword. The two baize-clad old men and the one who had served as guide to the boys then began pouring the wine from the cork vessel; but no sooner had they fallen to on the oranges than they were all startled by a loud knocking at the door. Ordering them to be calm, Monipodio went into the low room at the side and took down a shield, then drew his sword, came back to the door, and in a frightful hollow-sounding voice called out, "Who is there?"

"It is I," was the answer from without. "And I, Señor Monipodio, am nobody other than Tagarete.[29] I am on watch this morning, and I have come to tell you that Juliana with the chubby face is headed this way. Her hair is all down and she is crying as if something terrible had happened to her."

At that moment the woman came up, sobbing loudly, and when Monipodio heard her he opened the door and ordered Tagarete to go back to his post and not to make such an uproar the next time he came to report. The man promised to observe this admonition, and Chubby Face then came in. She was a girl of the same kind and profession as the other two. Her hair was streaming, her face was covered with bruises, and upon entering the patio she fell to the ground in a faint. Gananciosa and Escalanta ran to assist her,

and upon undoing her bosom they found that it was all black and blue as if it had been mangled. They then threw water on her and revived her.

"God's justice and the King's," she cried, "be upon that shameless thief, that cowardly sneak thief, that dirty scoundrel! I've saved him from the gallows more times than he has hairs in his beard. Poor me! Just see for what it is I have squandered the flower of my youth—for a wicked deceiver, an incorrigible villain like him!"

"Take it easy, Chubby Face," said Monipodio. "I am here, and I will see that justice is done you. Tell us how you have been wronged, and before you have finished I will avenge you. Have you had a falling out with your protector? [30] If that is the case, and it is revenge you want, you don't have to open your mouth."

"What a protector!" replied Juliana. "I'd rather be protected in hell than by that lion among lambs and lamb among men. Do you think I'm ever going to eat at the same table or sleep in the same bed with him again? Before I'd do that, I'd see this flesh devoured by jackals. Just look what he's done to me!" And, raising her skirts up to her knees or a little higher, she exhibited her legs, which were all covered with welts. "This is the kind of treatment I get from that ingrate of a Repolido,[31] who owes more to me than he does to the mother that bore him.

"And why do you think he did it? Was it on account of anything I had done? Certainly not. He was gambling and losing, and he sent Cabrillas, his runner, to ask me for thirty reales, and I only sent him twenty-four—may all the hard work and trouble I had in earning them be counted by Heaven against my sins! In repayment for this kindness on my part, thinking that I had more than I did and was holding out on him, he took me this morning and dragged me out into the fields behind the King's Garden, and there, among the olive trees, without even removing the iron buckles, he gave me such a flogging with his belt that he left me for dead. These welts that you see will bear witness to the truth of my story."

She now began screaming again, demanding justice, and again Monipodio and all the young bucks who were present promised that she should have it. Gananciosa took her hand to console her, saying that she herself would gladly give one of her most prized possessions if her own man had treated her the same way.

"For I must tell you, sister Chubby Face," she said, "if you do not know it already, punishment of that sort is a sign of love. When these ruffians beat and kick us, it is then that they most adore us. Come now, own up: after your Repolido had abused you like that, didn't he give you a caress?"

"Did he give me a caress?" said the weeping girl. "He gave me a hundred thousand, and he would have given a finger of his hand as well if I'd have gone with him to his lodgings. I even thought I could see the tears starting from his eyes after he had thrashed me like that."

"There is no doubt of it," said Gananciosa; "and he would weep with pain at seeing what he has done to you; for men like that, in such cases, have no sooner committed a fault than they are sorry for it. You will see, sister: he will come looking for you before we leave here and will ask your forgiveness for everything that has happened. He will be meek as a lamb."

"The truth is," said Monipodio, "that cowardly jailbird had better not set foot inside this door until he has done full penance for his crime. The nerve of him, laying his hands upon this girl's face or body! Why, when it comes to neatness and earnings, she can compete with Gananciosa here, and I can pay her no higher compliment than that!"

"Ay," exclaimed Juliana at this point, "don't be speaking ill of the poor fellow, Señor Monipodio, for however bad he may be, I love him with all my heart. The words that my friend Gananciosa just spoke in his behalf are the breath of life to me. As a matter of fact, I think I'll go look for him right now."

"Not if you take my advice," said Gananciosa, "for it will only make him feel puffed up and more important than ever, and he will treat you as he would a fencer's dummy. Calm yourself, sister, and before long, as I have said, you will see him coming in here full of repentance. If he does not come, we will make up some verses about him that will infuriate him."

"That we will," said Chubby Face, "for I have a thousand and one things to say to him."

"I will be the scribe, if necessary," said Monipodio; "for although I am not a poet by any means, if a man but roll up his sleeves to it he can turn out a couple of thousand couplets in no time at all; and if they are not all they ought to be, I have a barber friend, a great poet, who trims verses at all hours. But let us finish what we have begun by putting away this food, and afterward everything will be all right."

Juliana was content to obey her superior, and they all returned to their *gaudeamus* and within a short while had reached the bottom of the basket and the dregs of the flasks. The old men drank *sine fine*, the young men right heartily, and the ladies said their Kyrie eleisons.[32] The two elders then asked permission to leave, and Monipodio granted it, charging them to be sure to keep him informed of anything that the community ought to know. They promised to do so and went their way.

Being somewhat curious, Rinconete, after first begging Monipodio's pardon, asked him of what use two such old and dignified graybeards could be to the brotherhood. Monipodio replied that they were what were known in thieves' slang as "hornets," and that their business was to go through the city during the day and spy out houses that might be burglarized at night. They also followed those who drew money from the Bank of India or the Treasury, in order to see where it was taken and what was done with it. Having ascertained this, they tested the thickness of the walls of the house in question and marked the spot for the thieves to drill their *guzpátaros*, or holes, by means of which they effected an entrance. In short, he went on to say, they were quite as useful as any member of the brotherhood, if not more so, and received a fifth of whatever was stolen as a result of their efforts, just as His Majesty gets a fifth of any treasure that is found. They were, moreover, very truthful and upright individuals, God fearing and conscientious; they led model lives and enjoyed a good reputation.

"Some of them," he further explained, "especially the two who were here just now, are so accommodating that they are satisfied with much less than our rules allow them. We have another pair, a couple of porters who serve as furniture movers at times; they know the entrances and exits to all the houses in the city and which dwellings are worth our while and which are not."

"All that is wonderful, if you ask me," said Rinconete, "and I only hope that I can be of some use to this excellent fraternity."

"Heaven," said Monipodio, "always grants worthy desires." Just then there came another knock at the door, and he went over to see who was there.

"Open up, Señor Monipodio," came a voice in answer to his question, "it is I, Repolido."

"Don't let him in, your Grace!" cried Chubby Face when she heard this. "Don't open the door for that Tarpeian mariner, that tiger of Ocaña!" [33]

Monipodio paid no attention to her, however, and when she saw that Repolido was being admitted, she rose and ran into the room where the shields were, closing the door behind her.

"Get that ugly mug out of my sight!" she screamed from within. "I don't want to see that torturer of innocents, that frightener of tame doves!" [34]

Maniferro and Chiquiznaque held Repolido back, for he was determined to enter the room where Chubby Face was. Seeing that they would not let him go, he called out to her, "Stop it, little spitfire! For Heaven's sake, be quiet if you want to get married!"

"Get married, you rascal!" replied Chubby Face. "Just hear what he's harping on now! You'd like it all right if I'd take you, but I'd sooner marry a skeleton."

"That's enough, you little fool," said Repolido; "it's getting late. And don't let it turn your head to see me come to you so tame and meek, for, by the living God, if my anger mounts to the belfry, the relapse will be worse than the fall; so let's all come down off our high horses and not be giving the devil his dinner."

"I'd give him his supper too," said Chubby Face, "if only I never had to see you again."

"Didn't you hear what I said?" asked Repolido. "By God, Madame Strumpet, I'm losing my temper. I'll be putting them all out by the dozen, even though there's no sale." 35

"Let there be no rows in my presence," said Monipodio. "Chubby Face will come out not as a result of threats but because of her affection for me, and everything will be fine. When lovers quarrel, their pleasure is all the greater after they've made up. Come on out, Juliana my child, come out little Chubby Face, for my sake, and I will see to it that Repolido begs your forgiveness on his knees."

"Let him do that," said Escalanta, "and we will all be on his side and will insist on Juliana's coming out."

"If you expect me to humiliate myself," said Repolido, "a whole Swiss army couldn't force me to do that; but if it's to please Chubby Face, I may say that I'd not only get down on my knees but would drive a nail straight through my forehead to be of service to her."

Chiquiznaque and Maniferro laughed at this, at which Repolido, who thought they were making sport of him, became very angry. "If anyone," he said, "so much as thinks of laughing at anything that Chubby Face may say against me or I may say against her, I can tell him that he's a liar every time he does so." 36

Upon hearing this, Chiquiznaque and Maniferro exchanged such a dark look that Monipodio saw there would be trouble unless he took a hand.

"Do not go any further, gentlemen," he warned them. "Let us have no more of these insults; chew them up between your teeth, and so long as they do not reach the girdle,37 no one will be the worse for it."

"We are quite sure," replied Chiquiznaque, "that such threats

were not meant for us; for if we thought they were, the tambourine is in hands that know how to play it."

"We also have a tambourine, Sir Chiquiznaque," was Repolido's retort, "and we too, if necessary, can make the bells ring. I have said that whoever tries to make a joke out of this is a liar, and if anyone thinks otherwise, let him follow me, and with a sword that's shorter by a palm's length I will show him that I mean what I say."

With this, he started to go out the door. Chubby Face was listening, and when she heard how angry he was she came running out. "Stop him!" she cried. "Don't let him go or he'll be up to his old tricks! Can't you see what a temper he's in? Don't you know he's a Judas Macarelo [38] when he gets started? Come back here, you big bully! Come back, light of my eyes!" And laying hold of his cape, she tugged on it. Monipodio came to her assistance and between them they held him back. Chiquiznaque and Maniferro did not know whether to be offended or not and so remained quiet, waiting to see what he would do. Yielding to Chubby Face and Monipodio's entreaties, Repolido now turned. "Friends," he said, "ought not to provoke or make sport of each other, especially when they see that it is not being taken in good part."

"There is no one here," replied Maniferro, "who would want to provoke or make sport of a friend, and seeing that we are all friends, let's shake hands on it."

"Spoken like true friends," declared Monipodio, "and so, shake hands and let that be the end of it."

They did so at once. Escalanta took off one of her clogs and began drumming on it as if it had been a tambourine. Gananciosa snatched up a new palm-leaf broom that happened to be there and by scraping it produced a sound that, while harsh and unpleasing, went well enough with the one that came from the clog.[39] Monipodio broke a plate in two and, taking the pieces between his fingers, began rattling them with great dexterity, thereby providing a counterpoint. Rinconete and Cortadillo were quite astonished by this use to which the broom was put, for it was something they had never seen before.

"So that surprises you, does it?" said Maniferro. "Well it may, for there has never been an instrument invented that is so convenient and ready at hand or so cheap. In fact, I heard a student remark only the other day that neither Negrofeo, who brought Arauz up from hell, nor Marión, who mounted a dolphin and rose from the sea as if he were riding a hired mule, nor that other great musician who built a city that had a hundred gates and an equal number of posterns,[40] ever invented a better one, or one that you can pick up any time and is so easy to learn, since it has no frets, keys, or strings, and you don't have to bother about tuning it. They say it was the idea of a certain gallant of this city who prides himself on being a very Hector where music is concerned."

"That I can well believe," replied Rinconete; "but let's listen to our own musicians, for Gananciosa has just spit on the ground, and that's a sign she's getting ready to sing."

This proved to be the truth, for Monipodio had asked her to render a few popular *seguidillas*.[41] The first to begin, however, was Escalanta, in a small, quavering voice:

> "For a red-headed lad of old Seville,
> My heart is all aflame."

She was followed by Gananciosa:

"For a little brown lad I know, any girl
Would part with her good name."

Monipodio then began rattling his fragments of broken plate
in an energetic manner, and he too sang:

"Lovers may quarrel, but when peace is made,
Their loving pleasure grows."

Chubby Face also could not refrain from expressing her joy,
and she took off one of her own clogs and began a dance as an
accompaniment to the others:

"Then stop, for it is to your own flesh
You give these angry blows."

"Enough of that!" cried Repolido. "There's no sense in harping
on what's past and done, so take another theme and let bygones
be bygones."

The song they had begun might have lasted for some time if
it had not been for an urgent knock at the door. When Monipodio
went out to see who was there, the sentinel informed him that he
had caught sight of the magistrate down at the end of the street
and added that the officer was coming that way, preceded by
Grizzly and the Hawk, a couple of neutral constables.[42] Upon
hearing this, those inside were all greatly alarmed. Chubby Face
and Escalanta were so excited that they put on each other's clogs
and Gananciosa dropped her broom and Monipodio his im-
provised clappers. The music ceased, and silence fell on the
frightened assemblage. Chiquiznaque was dumb, Repolido was
scared, and Maniferro worried. Then everyone quickly disappeared from sight, some in one direction and some in another,
and ran up to the roofs and terraces in order to make their escape
by way of the other street.

Neither the sudden firing of a harquebus nor a clap of thunder out of a clear sky ever inspired such terror in a flock of careless pigeons as the unexpected arrival of the officer of the law did in all those good people gathered there. Rinconete and Cortadillo did not know what to do and accordingly remained where they were, waiting to see what the outcome of the squall would be. But the sentinel soon came back to say that the magistrate had gone on past without any sign of suspicion directed at their house.

As this report was being made to Monipodio, a young gentleman came up to the gate, dressed, as the saying goes, like a man about town.⁴³ Bringing the newcomer into the courtyard, Monipodio ordered Chiquiznaque, Maniferro, Repolido, and all the others to descend. Inasmuch as they had remained in the patio, Rinconete and Cortadillo were able to overhear the conversation that took place between the new arrival and his host. The young gentleman was asking Monipodio why they had made such a botch of the job he had ordered done. Monipodio replied that he did not know what the circumstances were but that the member charged with executing the job was present and would give a good account of himself. At that point Chiquiznaque came down, and his superior thereupon asked him if he had carried out the commission in question, a matter of a knife wound of fourteen stitches.

"Which one was that?" asked Chiquiznaque, "the merchant at the crossroads?"

"That's the one," said the gentleman.

"Well," said Chiquiznaque, "I will tell you what happened. I was waiting at night at the door of his house, and he came home shortly before time for prayers. I went up to him, took one look at his face, and saw that it was so small that a wound of fourteen stitches was out of the question; and not being able to keep my promise and follow destructions—"

"*Instructions,* your Grace means to say, not destructions," the gentleman corrected him.

"That was what I meant," said Chiquiznaque. "Well then, seeing that his face was too small and narrow for the required number of stitches, and not wishing to have my trip for nothing, I gave the cut to a lackey of his, and you can be sure that it was a first-rate one."

"I would rather," said the gentleman, "that you had given the master one of seven stitches than the servant one of fourteen. The short of it is, you have not complied with our agreement; but no matter, the thirty ducats that I left as down payment will be no great loss to me, and so I kiss your Grace's hands." Saying this, he took off his hat and turned to go, but Monipodio seized him by the cloak of varicolored cloth that he wore and drew him back.

"Just a moment," he said. "We have kept our word honorably and well, and you are going to have to do the same. You owe twenty ducats, and you're not leaving here until you pay or give us the equivalent in security."

"Is that what your Grace calls keeping your word," the gentleman demanded, "giving the cut to the servant instead of the master?"

"How well you get it!" exclaimed Chiquiznaque. "You don't seem to remember the proverb that says: 'He who loves Beltrán loves his dog.' " [44]

"But how does that proverb fit here?" said the gentleman.

"Why," Chiquiznaque went on, "isn't it the same thing as

saying: 'He who hates Beltrán hates his dog'? Beltrán is the merchant and you hate him; his lackey is his dog; by giving it to the dog you give it to Beltrán, the debt is wiped out, and we've accomplished our part. So there's nothing to do but settle the account."

"I will back him up in that," added Monipodio. "You took the words right out of my mouth, friend Chiquiznaque. As for you, Sir Gallant, don't be quibbling with your friends and servants but take my advice and pay for the work that's been done. If you would like for us to give the master another one of whatever size his face will hold, you may consider that they are already taking the stitches."

"In that case," replied the gallant, "I will gladly pay the entire cost for both of them."

"Have no doubt about it," Monipodio assured him, "but as you are a good Christian, believe me when I tell you that Chiquiznaque will leave so perfect a scar that people will think the fellow was born with it."

"In view of that assurance and your promise," said the gentleman, "take this chain as security for the twenty ducats I owe and the forty that I will pay you for the cut that is to come. By its weight it is worth a thousand reales, and it may be that it will remain in your hands, for I have an idea I am going to need another job of fourteen stitches before very long."

As he said this he removed from about his neck a chain made up of small links and gave it to Monipodio, who, upon running it through his fingers and weighing it in his hand, saw that it was no product of the alchemist. The leader of the gang was glad to have it and accepted it very politely, for he was extremely well bred. It was arranged that the job should be done that night by Chiquiznaque, and the gentleman then left well satisfied.

Calling all the absent ones down from the roof, Monipodio stood in the center of the group. He took out a memorandum book, which he carried in the hood of his cape, and gave it to Rinconete, as he himself did not know how to read. Upon opening it to the first page Rinconete found the following inscription:

MEMORANDUM OF SLASHES TO BE GIVEN THIS WEEK

" 'First, to the merchant of the crossroads; worth fifty crowns; thirty received on account. Secutor,[45] Chiquiznaque.' "

"That's all, son, I think," said Monipodio; "go on to where it says 'Memorandum of Thrashings.' "

Rinconete turned the page and on the following one found the entry. Beneath it was written: " 'To the alehouse keeper of Alfalfa Square, one dozen heavy blows at a crown each; eight on account. Time limit, six days. Secutor, Maniferro.' "

"You may as well cross that out," said Maniferro. "It will be taken care of tonight."

"Are there any more, son?" asked Monipodio.

"Yes," answered Rinconete, "there is one other that says: 'To the hunchback tailor, known as the Finch, six heavy blows at the request of the lady who left her necklace with him. Secutor, Lop-Eared.' "[46]

"I wonder," Monipodio mused, "why that hasn't been attended to. Lop-Eared must undoubtedly be sick, for it's two days beyond the time limit and it hasn't been carried out yet."

"I ran into him yesterday," said Maniferro, "and he told me that it was the hunchback who was home sick, which is the reason why it wasn't done."

"That I can well believe," said Monipodio, "for I know Lop-

Eared to be so good a worker that if there had not been some such reason he would have finished it at once. Are there any more, my lad?"

"No, sir," replied Rinconete.

"Then turn on," Monipodio directed him, "to where it says 'Memorandum of Common Outrages.'"

Rinconete turned the leaves until he came to this inscription:

MEMORANDUM OF COMMON OUTRAGES, NAMELY: THROWING OF VIALS; SMEARING WITH JUNIPER OIL; NAILING UP OF SAMBENITOS AND HORNS; PERSONS TO BE MOCKED IN PUBLIC; CREATING FALSE ALARMS AND DISTURBANCES; PRETENDED STABBINGS; CIRCULATION OF SLANDERS [47]

"And what does it say below?" asked Monipodio.

"It says," Riconete continued, " 'Smearing with juniper oil at the house of—' "

"Don't mention the house," said Monipodio, "for I know where it is. I am the *tu autem* and the executor in this trifling matter. Four crowns have already been paid against the total of eight."

"That's right," said Rinconete; "it's all written down here, and below it is, 'Nailing up of horns—' "

"Don't read that either," Monipodio again admonished him; "the house and the address do not matter. It is enough to commit the offense without speaking of it in public, for it is a great burden upon the conscience. I would rather nail up a hundred horns and as many sambenitos, providing I was paid for it, than mention the fact a single time even to the mother that bore me."

"The executor in this case," Rinconete informed him, "is Snub-nose."

"That has already been done and paid for," said Monipodio. "Look and see if there is anything else; for if I am not mistaken, there should be an alarm at twenty crowns, one-half down payment and our whole community as the executor; we have all this month in which to carry it out, and it shall be done without fail— it will be one of the biggest things that has happened in this town in a long while. Give me the book, lad. I know there's nothing else. Business is a bit slack just now, but times will change, and it may be we shall have more to do than we can take care of. There is not a leaf stirs without God's will, and we cannot force people to avenge themselves, especially seeing that everyone is now so brave in his own behalf that he doesn't want to pay for having something done that he can just as well do with his own hands."

"That is the way it is," said Repolido. "But, look, Señor Monipodio, let us know what your orders are, for it is getting late and the heat of the day is coming on very fast."

"What is to be done," said Monipodio, "is this. You are all to go to your posts and stay there until Sunday, when we will meet in this same place and divide everything that has fallen into our hands, without cheating anyone. Rinconete *the Good* [48] and Cortadillo will have for their district until the end of the week that part of the suburbs that lies between the Golden Tower and the Castle Postern. There they will have no trouble in working their tricks, for I have seen others that were not nearly so clever come back every day with more than twenty reales in small change, not to speak of the silver, and all this with only one deck and with four cards missing. Ganchuelo," he went on, addressing the youths, "will show you the lay of the land, and even though you go as far as San Sebastián and San Telmo, it will not make much difference, although it is only right that no one should trespass on another's territory."

The pair kissed his hand in return for the favor he had done them and promised to fulfill their tasks faithfully and well, with all diligence and discretion. Monipodio then took out from the hood of his cloak a folded sheet of paper containing a list of members and directed Rinconete to put down his own name and that of Cortadillo; but since they had no ink there, he told them they might take the paper with them and attend to the matter in the first apothecary's shop to which they came. The entry was to read: "Rinconete and Cortadillo, full members; apprenticeship, none; Rinconete, cardsharper; Cortadillo, sneak thief." They also were to note the day, month, and year, but were to say nothing about their parents or place of origin.

At this point one of the old men known as "hornets" arrived on the scene. "I have come," he said, "to inform your Graces that I just now met the young Wolf [49] of Malaga on the cathedral steps and he asked me to tell you that he is getting better at the business every day and that, with a clean deck, he could take the money from Satan himself. If he hasn't been around to report and render you obedience as usual, it is because he is so down and out, but he will be here Sunday without fail."

"I always did believe," said Monipodio, "that the Wolf would be outstanding in his line, for he has the best and cleverest pair of hands for it that anyone could wish. To be a good worker at a trade, you have to have good tools with which to practice it as well as the brains with which to learn it."

"I also," the old man continued, "ran into the Jew in a lodging house in the calle de Tintores. He was dressed like a priest and had gone there because he had heard that a couple of Peruvians were living in the house and he wished to see if he could get into a game with them, even though a small one at first, as it might amount to much more in the end. He also said that he would be sure to be at the meeting on Sunday and would give an account of himself."

"That Jew," said Monipodio, "is another good hawk and a very clever fellow; but I haven't seen him for days now, and that is not so good. I swear, if he doesn't watch his step, I'll fix him. That thief has no more holy orders than a Turk, and he doesn't know any more Latin than my mother. Anything else new?"

"No," answered the old man, "at least not that I know of."

"Very well then," said Monipodio, "here is a little something for you all." And with this he divided some forty reales among them. "Let no one fail to be here Sunday, and each one will get what's coming to him."

They all thanked him for his kindness, and the young couples embraced once more: Repolido and Chubby Face, Escalanta and Maniferro, and Gananciosa and Chiquiznaque. It was arranged that they should all meet that night at Pipota's house after they had finished the work in hand, and Monipodio remarked that he would also be there to make an inventory of the clothesbasket but that now he had to go and attend to the job of smearing with juniper oil. He embraced Rinconete and Cortadillo and dismissed them with his blessing, charging them that they should never have any permanent lodging or stopping place, as that was best for all concerned. Ganchuelo went with them to show them their post, and took occasion to remind them once again that they should not fail to put in an appearance on Sunday, since he believed that Monipodio intended to give them a lecture on things that had to do with their trade. He then went away, leaving the two lads quite astonished at all they had seen.

Although a mere boy, Rinconete had a naturally keen mind, and having accompanied his father in selling papal bulls, he knew something about the proper use of language. He had to laugh loudly as he thought of some of the words that Monipodio and the rest of that foolish community had employed. In place of *per modum suffragii* Monipodio had said *per modo de naufragio* ("by way of shipwreck"), and in speaking of the loot he had said *estupendo* in place of *estipendio*.[50] Then there was Chubby Face's remark that Repolido was like a "Tarpeian mariner," and a "tiger of Ocaña" (in place of Hyrcania), along with countless other silly things, of the same sort and even worse. (He was especially amused by her hope that the labor she had expended in earning the twenty-four reales would be counted by Heaven against her sins.)

Above all, he marveled at the absolute assurance they all felt of going to Heaven when they died so long as they did not fail in their devotions, and this in spite of all the thefts, murders, and other offenses of which they were guilty in the sight of God. He laughed also, as he thought of the old woman, Pipota, who, leaving the stolen hamper at home, went off to place her wax candles in front of the images; by doing so she doubtless was convinced that she would go to Heaven fully clothed and with her shoes on. He was no less astonished at the obedience and respect they all showed Monipodio, that coarse, unscrupulous barbarian. He recalled what he had read in the latter's memorandum book of the practices in which they were all engaged. And, finally, he was astounded by the careless manner in which justice was administered in that famous city of Seville, with people so pernicious as these and possessed of such unnatural instincts carrying on their pursuits almost openly.

He made up his mind to persuade his companion that they should not continue long in this desperate and evil way of life, one so free and dissolute and marked by such uncertainty. But in spite of it all, being young and inexperienced, he did continue in it for a number of months, and in the course of that time had certain adventures which it would take too long to set down here. Accordingly, we must wait for another occasion to hear the story of his life and the strange things that happened to him, as well as to his teacher Monipodio, along with other events having to do with the members of that infamous academy, all of which should be very edifying and well might serve as an example and a warning to those who read.

MAN OF GLASS

Man of Glass

A couple of students were riding along the banks of the river Tormes when they came upon a lad sleeping beneath a tree. He was around eleven years of age and dressed like a peasant. Having sent a servant to awaken him, they asked him from where it was he came and what he meant by falling asleep in a lonely spot like that. The lad's answer was that he had forgotten the name of his native province, and was bound for the city of Salamanca to look for a master whom he might serve, but on one condition, that he be permitted to continue his studies. They then inquired if he knew how to read, and he assured them that he not only could read but could also write.

"In that case," said one of the gentlemen, "it is not through any lapse of memory that you have forgotten the name of your birthplace."

"Be that as it may," replied the youth, "no one shall know of it, nor shall they know the name of my parents, until I am in a position to reflect honor on them and it."

"And in what manner do you propose to reflect honor on them?" asked the other gentleman.

"Through the fame that I acquire for my learning," said the boy, "for I have heard it said that out of men bishops are made."

As a result of this reply the two travelers decided to take the lad along with them, and when they arrived at their destination, they allowed him to begin studying; for it is a custom in that university to permit servants to do so.[1] He told them that his name was Tomás Rodaja,[2] which led his masters to infer, by reason of the name and the manner in which he was clad, that he was the son of some poor peasant. Within a few days they had dressed him in a black robe, and in the course of a few weeks he gave evidence of possessing a mind that was quite out of the ordinary. He served his employers so loyally, diligently, and conscientiously that, while in nowise neglecting his books, he gave the impression of being solely concerned with waiting upon them.

And since a good servant is likely to win good treatment from his master, Tomás Rodaja soon became more of a companion to them than anything else. The short of it is that during the eight years he remained with them he became so famous in the university, by reason of his fine intellect and outstanding abilities, that people of all sorts were led to love and esteem him. His principal study was the law, but where he shone most brightly was in the field of literature and the humanities. Fortunately, he had an astonishing memory, and this as well as the keen intelligence he displayed contributed to his reputation.

At length the time came when his masters had finished their

own studies and were ready to return to their home, which was in one of the largest cities in Andalusia. They took Tomás with them, and he stayed there a few days, but it was not long before he felt a great desire to return to his books at Salamanca—a desire that is shared by all those who once have tasted of the pleasant way of life that city affords—and he accordingly asked the gentlemen for permission to leave them. Being courteous and generous-minded, they granted his request and provided for him so well that he was able to live for three whole years on what they gave him.

Expressing his thanks to them, Tomás said good-by and left Malaga, which was the city in which his masters lived; and as he was descending the Zambra slope on the road to Antequera, he fell in with a gentleman on horseback who was gaily clad for the road [3] and was accompanied by two servants, also mounted. Upon joining his new acquaintance, he learned that the latter was going in the same direction, and so they became traveling companions. They spoke of various things, with Tomás revealing his rare qualities of mind while the other gave proof of gallantry and good breeding. The gentleman stated that he was a captain of infantry in the service of His Majesty, and that his ensign was at that moment engaged in recruiting a company in the neighborhood of Salamanca. He went on to praise the life of a soldier, giving a vivid description of the beauty of Naples, the merrymakings of Palermo, the abundance of good things to be found at Milan, the feastings of Lombardy, and the splendid meals to be had in the hostelries. He politely and carefully explained the meaning of such expressions as "*Aconcha, patrón; passa acá, manigoldo; venga la macarela, li polastri e li macarroni.*" [4]

He extolled to the sky the freedom that soldiers enjoyed in Italy, but said nothing about the cold of sentry duty, the danger that lay in an attack, the terror of battles, the hunger endured in a siege, the destruction wrought by mines, or other things of that sort, although there are some who look upon these burdensome accompaniments of the military life as constituting its chief characteristic. In short, he talked so long and so well that Tomás Rodaja's judgment began to waver, and the lad came to feel an attraction for this way of life which is always so near to death.

Being extremely well pleased with the boy's good appearance, his qualities of mind, and his manners, Don Diego de Valdivia (for that was the captain's name) invited Tomás, in case he was desirous of seeing Italy, to come along with him and share his mess, adding that, if necessary, he could make the youth his standard bearer, as his ensign was thinking of leaving him shortly. It did not require much urging for Tomás to accept the bid,[5] for he quickly reflected that it would be a very good thing to have a glimpse of Italy and Flanders and various other lands and countries, since long journeys of this sort made men wise. This one at the most would require but three or four years, he was still young, and it would not prevent him from returning to his studies later.

He appeared bent, however, upon having everything to suit his own wishes, and told the captain that he would be glad to accompany him to Italy but that it would have to be on condition that he was not to be compelled to serve under any banner or have his name entered on the regimental rolls, as he wished to come and go as he liked. The captain replied that his being on the rolls would not make any difference as he might have leave whenever he asked for it, and that way might draw the same pay and receive the same treatment as other members of the company.

"But that," said Tomás, "would go against my conscience and against yours as well, *Señor Capitán,* and accordingly I would rather come as a free man than be under any obligations."

"So scrupulous a conscience as yours," remarked Don Diego, "is the sort one would expect to find in a monk rather than a soldier; but have it your way, for we are comrades in any event."

They reached Antequera, and within a few days, by means of long journeys, they overtook the company, which had now been recruited and was ready to set out on the march to Cartagena. It was joined by four other companies, the men being billeted in any villages through which they happened to pass. Tomás now had a chance to observe the overbearing attitude of the commissaries, the bad temper of some of the captains, the graspingness of the quartermasters, the manner in which the paymasters kept their accounts, the resentment of the people in the villages, the traffic in lodgings, the insolence of the recruits, the quarrels with guests at the inn, and the requisitioning of more supplies than were needed. He also perceived that it was almost impossible to avoid falling in with these ways, which impressed him as being neither right nor just.

By this time Tomás was dressed like a popinjay,[6] having laid aside the garb of a student and put on that of "God is Christ," [7] as the saying goes. Of all the books he had previously owned he retained but two, one of them a collection of prayers to Our Lady, and the other a Garcilaso,[8] without notes, both of which he carried in his pockets. They arrived all too soon at Cartagena, for life in the camps afforded a wide variety of experiences and every day there was something new to be seen and enjoyed. The troops then embarked in four galleys bound for Naples, and Tomás had a chance to study the strange life that goes on inside these maritime houses, where most of the time one is eaten alive by bedbugs, devoured by rats, robbed by the galley slaves, annoyed by the crew, and sickened by the roll of the waves. He was frightened by the great storms and tempests, especially two that they encountered in the Gulf of Lions, one of which cast them ashore on the island of Corsica, while the other drove them back to Toulon in France.

At last, gaunt, weary, and soaked to the skin, they arrived at the exceedingly lovely city of Genoa, where they disembarked in the little basin known as the Mandraccio.[9] After having visited a church, the captain and all his comrades repaired to a hostelry where they proceeded to forget past squalls by celebrating their present joy. It was then they came to know the smooth taste of Trebbiano, the full body of Montefiascone, the sharp tang of Asprino, the hearty flavor of those two Greek wines, Candia and Soma, the strength of Five Vineyards, the sweetness and charm of Lady Vernaccia, and the rude bite of Centola, all of which were such lordly vintages that the lowly Romanesco did not care to show its face among them.[10]

After their host had familiarized them with this great variety of wines, he offered to produce before them, not by any sleight of hand or as if painted on a map, but really and truly, such other brands as Madrigal, Coca, Alaejos, and that imperial rather than Royal City,[11] which is the abode of the god of laughter. He gave them their choice of Esquivias, Alanís, Cazalla, Guadalcanal, and Membrilla, not forgetting Ribadavia and Descargamaría.[12] To make a long story short, he named and set before them more wines than Bacchus himself could possibly have in all his vaults.

The worthy Tomás also admired the blond hair of the Genoese lasses and the courteous and lively disposition of the men, as well

as the marvelous beauty of the city itself, whose houses, perched high on the cliffs, looked like diamonds set in gold. The next day all the companies that were to go to the Piedmont left the ship. Tomás, however, did not care to make this journey, preferring to go by way of land to Rome and Naples, which he did, his intention being to return by way of the great city of Venice and Loretto to Milan and from there to the Piedmont, where Don Diego de Valdivia said that he would be in case he had not already gone on to Flanders.

Two days later Tomás bade farewell to the captain, and in five days arrived at Florence, having first visited Lucca, a small city but very well constructed, where Spaniards were better regarded and better received than in other parts of Italy. He was greatly pleased with Florence, not only by reason of its charming site, but also because of its cleanliness, its magnificent buildings, its cool-flowing river, and the tranquility of its streets. He remained there four days, then departed for Rome, that queen of cities and mistress of the world. He visited its temples, adored its relics, and marveled at its grandeur. Just as from the claws of a lion one may judge the size and ferocity of the beast, so was his opinion of Rome formed from its marble ruins, the statuary whether whole or mutilated, its crumbling arches and baths, its magnificent porticoes, and huge amphitheaters, the renowned and sacred river that washes its banks to the brim and blesses them with countless relics from the bodies of martyrs that are buried there, its bridges which appear to be admiring one another, and its streets whose very names invest them with a dignity beyond those of all other cities in the world: the Via Appia, the Via Flaminia, the Via Julia, and others of that sort.

He was no less pleased by the manner in which the city was

divided by its hills: the Caelian, the Quirinal, and the Vatican, along with the other four whose names show forth the greatness and majesty that is Rome.[13] He likewise remarked the authority that is exerted by the College of Cardinals, as well as the majesty of the Supreme Pontiff and the great variety of peoples and nations that are gathered there. He saw and made note of everything and put everything in its proper place. Having done the stations of the seven churches [14] and confessed himself to a penitentiary father and kissed the foot of His Holiness, being by then laden down with *Agnus Dei's* and beads, he made up his mind to go on to Naples; and inasmuch as it was the dog days, a bad and dangerous time for entering or leaving Rome, and since he had made the journey thus far by land, he decided now to take the boat. If he had marveled at what he saw in Rome, he marveled still more when he reached his destination; for Naples impressed him, as it does all those who have had a sight of it, as being the best city in Europe and even in all the world.

From there he proceeded to Sicily, visiting Palermo, and afterward Messina. The former impressed him by the beauty of its location, the latter by its harbor, while the whole island was a cause for wonderment on account of the great abundance of its products, which has led, and rightly so, to its being called the storehouse of Italy.

After returning to Naples he went on to Rome, and from there to Our Lady of Loretto, in whose holy shrine he was unable to see either walls or partitions, for the reason that they were wholly covered with crutches, shrouds, chains, shackles, manacles, locks of hair, wax figures, paintings, and altarpieces, all of which was a clear indication of the innumerable favors that many had received from the hand of God through the intercession of His

Divine Mother, whose most holy image He wished to honor and dignify through a multitude of miracles as a recompense for the devotion represented by those votive offerings that adorned the walls of Her chapel. He also saw the room and chamber that had witnessed the loftiest and most important embassy that all the angels in all the heavens and all the inhabitants of the eternal dwelling places had ever seen or heard.[15]

At Ancona he took ship and went on to Venice, a city that, if Columbus had never been born into this world, would have had no equal; but thanks to Heaven and to the great Hernando Cortés, who conquered the great land of Mexico, Venice the great now has, in a manner of speaking, a worthy rival. These two famous cities have streets that consist wholly of water, the one being the wonder of the Old World, while the other is the marvel of the New.[16] It seemed to him that the riches of Venice were infinite, its government prudent, its site inexpugnable, its abundance a cause for wonderment, its surroundings most pleasant; in short, everything in it was worthy of the fame that it enjoyed throughout the world, a fame that was increased by its famous shipyard, where its galleys and other vessels without number were constructed.

The pleasures and pastimes that our student found here in Venice almost equaled those of Calypso and came near causing him to forget his original intention; but after he had been there for a month, he returned by way of Ferrara, Parma, and Piacenza to Milan, that workshop of Vulcan and envy of the King of France, a city, in brief, of which it is commonly remarked that saying is equivalent to doing,[17] its magnificence being due to the grandeur of its cathedral and the marvelous abundance that is to be found there of all the things that are necessary to human life.

From there he journeyed to Asti, arriving the day before the regiment was to leave. He was very well received by his friend the captain and continued with him to Flanders as his close friend and comrade, in due time reaching Antwerp, a city no less filled with wonders than those he had seen in Italy. He also had a sight of Ghent and Brussels and perceived that the whole country was ready to take up arms and begin the campaign the following summer.

Having seen the things that he desired to see, he then made up his mind to return to Spain and complete his studies at Salamanca; and this at once he proceeded to do, to the very great regret of his comrade, who, when the time for departure came, begged the young man to send back word as to his safe arrival, state of health, and how things were going with him. Promising to do all this, Tomás made his way back to Spain by way of France, but without seeing Paris, which was then up in arms. Upon reaching Salamanca and being warmly welcomed by his friends, he resumed his studies with their assistance until he was graduated as a licentiate in law.

Now as it happened, there came to the city at this time a lady of great worldly experience who was deeply versed in feminine wiles, and at once all the birds of the place came flocking in response to her decoys and enticements, and there was not a single *vademecum* [18] who did not call upon her. Having been told that the lady in question had been in Italy and Flanders, and wishing to see if he knew her, Tomás likewise paid her a visit, and as a result she fell in love with him. He, however, did not reciprocate this feeling, and indeed refused to go to her house unless forcibly taken there by others. Finally she revealed her love to him and offered him what property she had; but inasmuch as he was more concerned with his books than with pastimes of this sort, he did not give her any encouragement whatever.

Seeing herself thus disdained and, as she thought, despised, and realizing that she would not be able to overcome his rocklike determination by any ordinary means, she resolved to employ a method that would be more efficacious and lead to the fulfillment of her desires. And so, upon the advice of a Moorish woman, she put one of those so-called love potions into a Toledan quince [19] and gave it to Tomás, believing that this would force him to care for her, just as if there were in this world herbs, enchantments, or magic words sufficient to sway the free will of any individual. Those who give such potions are rightly called poisoners, for it is really nothing other than poison that they purvey to their victims, as experience has shown upon many and various occasions.

Tomás ate the quince and was at once so violently affected by it that he began to shake from head to foot as if in an epileptic fit. He did not recover for many hours, and when he did, he appeared to be stupefied, and with a thickened tongue was only able to stammer that it was the quince that was responsible for his condition. He told them who the person was who had given it to him, and the law at once took a hand in the case; but when the officers went to look for the guilty party, they found that she, having learned how things had turned out, had taken to cover, and nothing more was heard of her after that.

For six months Tomás was in bed, and in the course of that time he withered away and became, as the saying goes, nothing but skin and bones, while all his senses gave evidence of being deranged. His friends applied every remedy in their power and succeeded in curing the illness of his body but not that of his mind, with the result that he was left a healthy man but afflicted with the strangest kind of madness that had ever been heard of up to that time. The poor fellow imagined that he was wholly made of glass, and consequently, when anyone came near him, he would give a terrible scream, begging and imploring them with the most rational-sounding arguments to keep their distance lest they shatter him, since really and truly he was not like other men but was fashioned of glass from head to foot.

In an effort to cure him of this weird delusion, many paid no attention to his cries and entreaties but came up to him and embraced him, telling him to take a look and he would see that he had not been broken; but the only effect of this was to cause the poor man to throw himself to the ground screaming harder than ever, after which he would lose consciousness for four solid hours. When he came to himself, it was only to beg and plead with them not to do it again. Let them converse with him from afar, he urged, in which case they might ask him anything they liked and he would answer all questions that were put to him as intelligently as anyone could wish, considering that he was a man of glass and not of flesh. The fact was, he asserted, that glass, being a thin and delicate material, enabled the soul to act more promptly and efficiently than could a heavy earthen body.

Some wished to try an experiment to see if he spoke the truth, and they plied him with many difficult questions, to all of which he immediately replied with a display of the keenest intelligence. Even among the learned of the university, including the professors of medicine and philosophy, great astonishment was created upon seeing that an individual so extraordinarily mad as to believe that he was made of glass could still possess so profound an understanding of things that he was able to give the proper answer, and a perspicacious one, on any subject.

Tomás then asked them to furnish him with some kind of sheath for the fragile vase of his body, lest in drawing on a tight-fitting garment he might break himself, and they accordingly provided him with a dark-colored robe and a very wide chemise, in which he clothed himself with the greatest caution, employing a strand of cotton as a girdle; but he would not even consider putting on a pair of shoes. When it came to eating, they had to hand him his food on the end of a stick, in a little straw basket in which they placed whatever fruit was in season. He would have neither meat nor fish and drank only from the fountain or the river by lapping up the water with his hands. When he went out he always walked in the middle of the street, gazing up all the while at the roof-tops, for he was afraid that some tile might fall upon him. In summer he slept in the open air, out in the fields, and in winter he went to some tavern and buried himself in straw up to the neck, re-marking that this was the only proper bed and the safest one for men of glass. When it thundered he trembled like quicksilver and would run out into the fields and not come back to town until the storm had passed.

His friends kept him shut up much of the time; but when they saw that he was getting no better, they decided to yield to his wishes and let him go about freely. When he made his appear-ance in the city, all who knew him were astonished and sym-pathized with him. The small boys surrounded him, but he held them off with his staff and urged them not to come near, saying that, being a man of glass, he was very delicate and brittle and they might readily break him. Young lads, however, are the most mischievous creatures in the world, and despite his screams and entreaties they began throwing stones and other objects at him to see if he really was made of glass as he insisted; but he cried so loudly and made such a fuss that adults came running up to scold the lads and punish them so that they would not do it again. One day when the urchins were annoying him more than usual he turned upon them.

"Listen, you boys," he said, "persistent as flies, filthy as bedbugs, bold as fleas, am I by any chance the Monte Testaccio of Rome [20] that you should be throwing all these tiles and pieces of crockery at me?"

Since they enjoyed hearing his replies and his scoldings, the young ones continued to follow him about, until they came to prefer listening to him to throwing things at him.

He had other experiences as well. As he was walking through the garment district of Salamanca on one occasion, a shopkeeper's wife said to him, "Upon my soul, Señor Licentiate, I am sorry for the trouble you are in, but what can I do, seeing that I cannot weep?" [21] He thereupon turned to her and in measured tones replied, *"Filiae Hierusalem: plorate super vos et super filios vestros."* [22] Hearing this malicious remark, the woman's husband spoke up. "Brother Glasscase,[23] for they tell me that is what they call you, I think you are more of a rogue than a madman."

"It doesn't make a penny's worth of difference," came the reply, "but I can tell you that I am no fool."

Chancing one day to pass the brothel or common inn, he saw many of the inmates standing in the doorway and told them that they were the baggage of Satan's army, lodged in hell's own hostelry. Another time, someone asked him what advice should be given to a friend who was very sad because his wife had gone away with another man. In this case the answer was: "Tell him to give thanks to God for having permitted the other man to carry off his enemy."

"Then he is not to go look for her?"

"Let him not think of it," replied Glasscase, "for if he finds her, what he really will find will be a veritable and perpetual witness to his own dishonor."

"That being so," said the stranger, "what should I do to keep peace with my own wife?"

"Provide her with whatever she needs and allow her to give orders to all those of her household but never to you."

"Señor Glasscase," said a boy, "I'd like to get away from my father, for he is all the time beating me."

"Remember, my child, that the lashes that fathers give their sons are an honor; it is those of the public executioner that are a disgrace."

Standing at the door of a church, he saw a peasant going in, one of those who are forever priding themselves on being old Christians, and behind him came one who was not in such good standing; whereupon, addressing the peasant, the licentiate called out in a loud voice, "Wait, Domingo, until Sabado has passed." [24] He also had his say as to schoolmasters, observing that they were fortunate in that they were always dealing with little angels, and especially so if the cherubs in question did not happen to be little snotnoses. Yet another asked him what he thought of whores, and he replied that the real whores were not the ones so called, but rather neighbor women. [25]

The news of his madness, his replies, and his sayings had by now spread throughout Castile and had reached the ears of a personage high at court who wished to have him brought there and who charged a friend in Salamanca to send him on. This gentleman, happening to meet the licentiate one day, said to him, "I may tell you, Señor Glasscase, that an important personage at the court wishes to see you and has sent for you." To this the licentiate replied, "Your Grace will please tell that gentleman that I wish to be excused, since I am not adapted to palace life, for I have a sense of shame and am not good at flattery."

Nevertheless, the Salamancan did send him to the court, and by way of transporting him there made use of the following contrivance: they placed him in a straw pannier well balanced with stones on both sides, of the sort that are used for carrying glass, and amidst the straw they placed a few bottles by way of showing that it was glass that was being thus conveyed. Upon reaching Valladolid,[26] they made their entrance by night and removed the licentiate from the basket at the home of the gentleman who had wanted to see him and who now gave him a very pleasant reception, saying, "You are heartily welcome, Señor Glasscase. And what kind of a journey did you have? How is your health?"

"No journey," replied the licentiate, "is a bad one that brings you to your destination, unless it be the one that leads to the gallows. As to my health, I have nothing of which to complain, seeing that my pulse is on good terms with my brain."

The next day, having seen many perches on which were numerous falcons, goshawks, and other birds that are used in fowling, he remarked that falconry was a sport suited to princes and great lords, but that it was to be noted that the expense exceeded the profit that was to be had from it by a ratio of more than two thousand to one. The hunting of hares, he added, was good sport, especially when one made use of borrowed hounds. The gentleman was amused by this display of madness and permitted his guest to go about the city with one man as a bodyguard, to see to it that the boys did not harm him; for he was known to them and

to all the court within a week's time, and in each street, at every step he took, and on every corner where he stopped, he had to answer the questions that were put to him. Among those who questioned him was a student, who inquired if he was a poet, since he appeared to have a mind that was apt for anything.

"Up to now," replied the licentiate, "I have been neither so foolish nor so bold."

"I do not understand what you mean by those words, foolish and bold," said the student; and Glasscase then went on to explain, "I have never been so foolish as to be a bad poet nor so bold as to think that I could be a good one."

When another student asked him what opinion he held of poets, he answered by saying that he had a high respect for the science of poetry but none for poets themselves; and when they wished to know what he meant by that, he went on to say that of the infinite number of poets in the world there were so few good ones that they were practically negligible; and thus, since there were no poets to speak of, he could not esteem them, though he admired and reverenced the science of poetry, which contains within itself all the other sciences, makes use of all of them, adorns itself with them, and cleanses them, while bringing to light its own marvelous works that fill the world with profit, delight, and wonderment.

"I am quite aware," he continued, "of the esteem in which a good poet is to be held, for I remember those verses of Ovid where he says:

> 'Cura ducum fuerunt olim regumque poetae,
> premiaque antiqui magna tulere chori,
> sanctaque maiestas, et erat venerabile nomen
> vatibus, et largae saepe dabantur opes. . .'

Nor am I oblivious to the great worth of poets, whom Plato has called the interpreters of the gods, and of whom Ovid says:

'Est Deus in nobis; agitante calescimus illo.'

And there is that other verse of his:

'At sacri vates, et divum cura vocamus.' [27]

This is said of the good poets, but what of the bad ones, the poetasters? What is there to say except that they are the most stupid and arrogant tribe in all the world?

"Did you ever observe one of these latter as he gave a first reading of a sonnet to a company of people? If so, you must have noticed the ceremony that he makes of it as he says, 'I should like your Graces to listen to a little sonnet that I composed one night. While it is only a trifle, I think it is rather good.' And with this he twists his lips, arches his brows, fumbles in his pocket, and from among countless soiled and half-torn scraps of paper containing numerous other sonnets, he brings forth the one that he wishes to recite and finally proceeds to read it in a honeyed, sugary tone of voice. And if his listeners, either out of malice or out of ignorance, fail to praise it, he will say, 'Oh, but your Graces surely failed to hear my sonnet, or else I did not read it properly, and so, I think, it would be well for me to recite it once more; and I hope your Graces will pay greater attention this time, as it is really quite worth your while.' And he will read it once more with fresh gestures and new pauses.

"Then, what a thing it is to hear them when they start criticizing one another! And what shall one say of the thefts that these modern whelps commit upon the grave and ancient mastiffs of their art? What is to be said of those that are always carping at cer-

tain illustrious ones of outstanding ability in whom the true light
of poetry shines resplendent and who, adopting this pursuit as
a relief and relaxation from their many serious occupations, continue to exhibit their lofty conceptions and a truly divine inspira-
tion in spite of the ignorant onlooker who passes judgment upon
something of which he knows nothing and abhors that which he
does not understand? What of the self-esteem of the one who
prides himself upon his own foolishness and would take his place
beneath the canopy of fame, or the ignorance that would sit in
the seat of the mighty?"

On another occasion they asked him why it was that most poets
were poor, and he replied that it was because they chose to be,
since they had it in their power to be rich if they only knew how
to make use of the wealth that lay in their hands at times—namely,
that of their ladies, who were all exceedingly opulent in golden
locks, brows of burnished silver, eyes that were green emeralds,
teeth of ivory, coral lips, and throats of transparent crystal, while
their tears were liquid pearls; and, moreover, the very ground
they trod, though it might be hard and sterile earth, at once produced jasmine and roses. Was not the food they ate of purest
amber, musk, and civet, and were not all these things the sign
and evidence of great wealth? All this and more he had to say of
the bad poets, but he always spoke well of the good ones, elevat-
ing them above the horns of the moon.

One day, in the San Francisco walk, he came upon some
badly painted figures and observed that good painters imitate
nature but bad ones vomit it forth.[28] On another occasion, carefully feeling his way for safety's sake, he came up to a bookseller's shop and said to the proprietor, "This trade would please
me very much, if it were not for one vice connected with it."

When the bookseller asked him what that vice was, he answered, "The tricks that you play when you purchase the rights to a book and the sport that you make of an author if by chance he has it printed at his own cost; for in place of fifteen hundred copies, you go ahead and print three thousand, and while the author thinks that it is his copies that are being sold, it is in reality your own that you are getting rid of."

That same day six criminals who were to be flogged passed through the square, and when the crier called out, "The first one for being a thief—" the licentiate raised his voice and addressed those in front of him, saying, "Take care, brothers, that he doesn't call out the name of one of you." And when the crier came to the word "hindermost," Glasscase remarked, "He must be referring to the bondsman of young lads." [29] One boy thereupon said to him, "Brother Glasscase, they are going to flog a whore," and he answered, "If you had told me it was a pimp they were going to flog I would have understood you to mean that they were going to flog a coach." [30]

Among the other bystanders was a litter bearer, and it was he who put the next question. "How comes it, Sir Licentiate, have you nothing to say of us?"

"No," replied Glasscase, "I have nothing to say, unless it be that each one of you knows more sins than a father confessor, but with this difference: the confessor knows them in order to keep them secret, and you, in order that you may make them public in all the taverns."

One of those lads with mules for hire happened to hear this; for all sorts of people were constantly standing around listening to the licentiate. "Señor Vial," the lad asked, "how does it come that you have had little or nothing to say about us, although we are good people and necessary to the life of the state?" Glasscase had an answer for him. "The honor of the servant," he said, "depends upon that of the master; and so, just look and see whom it is you serve, and you will see how much honor you possess. They are the filthiest trash to be found anywhere on this earth. Once upon a time, before I became a man of glass, I made a journey on a hired mule, and I counted in them one hundred and twenty-one capital defects, inimical to the human race. All you lads have in you something of the pimp, something of the thief, and something of the mountebank. If your masters (for such is the name you give to those you carry upon your mules) chance to be simpletons, you play more tricks on them than this city has known for many years past; if they are foreigners, you rob them; if they are students, you curse them; if they are religious, you blaspheme against them; and if they are soldiers, you tremble from fear.

"You fellows, along with sailors, carters, and pack carriers, lead a life that is all your own and one of a most extraordinary kind. The carter spends his days within the space of a yard and a half, for it cannot be more than that from the yoke of his mules to the front of his cart. Half the time he is singing and the other half he is cursing or yelling 'Get behind there!' when someone tries to pass him. And if by any chance he has to stop to get one of his wheels out of a rut, two good round oaths are of more use to him than three mules.

"Sailors are a fine lot, though unversed in city ways, and they know no other language than that which is used aboard ship. In fair weather they are diligent, but they are lazy in a storm. In a tempest they give many orders and obey few. Their god is their seamen's chest and their grub, and they find amusement in watching the seasick passengers.

"As for the carriers, they have been divorced from sheets and have married packsaddles. They are so industrious and have such an eye for business that they would lose their souls rather than a day's haul. Their music is that of hoofs, their sauce is hunger, their matins consist in speaking their mind, and they go to mass by hearing none."

As he said this, he was standing at the door of an apothecary's shop, and, turning to the proprietor, he observed, "Your Grace has a wholesome occupation, if it were not that it is so bad for your lamps."

"How is it bad for my lamps?" the apothecary wanted to know.

"I say so," replied Glasscase, "for the reason that, whenever you happen to be in need of oil, you supply it from the lamp that is nearest at hand. And there is another thing about this business that is enough to ruin the reputation of the best doctor in the world." When asked what it was, he went on to explain that there were certain apothecaries who, when they did not have on hand what the physician prescribed, would substitute other drugs which they believed to possess the same qualities and healing properties. This was not so, however, and the result was that the prescription, badly compounded, had exactly the opposite effect.

Someone then asked him what he thought of doctors, and his reply was, " '*Honora medicum propter necessitatem, etenim creavit eum Altissimus. A Deo enim est omnis medela, et a rege accipiet donationem. Disciplina medici exaltabit caput illius, et in conspectu magnatum collaudabitur. Altissimus de terra creavit medicinam, et vir prudens non abhorrebit illam.*' [31] That is what Ecclesiasticus has to say of medicine and of good doctors, and just the reverse might be said of the bad ones, for there is no class of people more dangerous to the state than they. The judge

may pervert or delay justice; the man of law may in his own interest plead an unjust cause; the merchant may drain off our
property—in short, all those with whom we must necessarily deal
may do us some wrong, but there is none of them other than the
doctor who is in a position to deprive us of life itself, without
punishment.

"Physicians may and do kill without fear or running away and
without unsheathing any other sword than that of a prescription;
for there is no means of discovering their crimes, since they at
once bury them underground. I recall something that happened
when I was a man of flesh and not of glass as I am today. A doctor
of the kind I have been speaking of sent a patient of his to another
physician for treatment, and three or four days later, upon passing the shop of the apothecary who filled the other doctor's pre-
scriptions, he looked in and inquired if his colleague had prescribed some purge or other. The apothecary replied that, as a
matter of fact, he did have such a prescription for a purge, which
the patient was to take the following day. The first doctor then
asked that it be shown to him, and down at the bottom he saw the
words: *Sumat diluculo*.[32] 'That,' he said, 'seems to me a very
good remedy. The only thing I am in doubt about is the *diluculo*,
as it contains a little too much moisture.' "

By reason of this and other things he had to say concerning all
the trades and professions, a crowd always followed him about but
did him no injury though he was never left in peace. He would
not, however, have been able to ward off the small boys if his
bodyguard had not been there to protect him.

Someone asked him what to do in order to avoid envying another, and he replied, "Sleep; for all the time that you are asleep
you will be the equal of the one you envy." Another who for a

couple of years had been seeking a commission wanted to know what he should do to make things come out right; and the answer this time was, "Mount your horse, and when you see someone bearing such a commission, accompany him until he leaves the city, and you will come out with the thing you desire." [33]

As he stood there in the street a judge went by on his way to a criminal trial, accompanied by two bailiffs and a large crowd of people. "I will wager," said Glasscase upon being informed who it was, "that this judge has vipers in his bosom, pistols in his inkpot, and thunderbolts in his hand to destroy everything that comes within his jurisdiction. I recall once having had a friend in the same position who, in connection with a case that came up before him, imposed so unreasonable a sentence that it exceeded by many carats the guilt of the offenders. When I asked him why he had done this, thereby committing so obvious an injustice, he told me that he expected the case to be appealed and that in this way he was leaving the field open for the gentlemen of the Council to show mercy by moderating this harsh sentence and imposing in its stead one that was proportionate to the crime. I remarked that it would have been better if he had spared them the trouble of doing so, since then he would have been looked upon as a wise and upright magistrate."

In the circle of listeners that constantly surrounded him was an acquaintance of his in the garb of an advocate whom the others addressed as "Señor Licentiate," though Glasscase was aware that the man held no other degree than that of bachelor.[34] "You had better watch out, my friend," he said to him, "or the Redemptionist Friars will pick you up and confiscate that title of yours as strayed or stolen property." [35]

"Come, Señor Glasscase," said his friend, "that is no way to talk; you know very well that I am a man of lofty and profound learning."

"I know," answered Glasscase, "that you are a very Tantalus when it comes to learning, seeing that it is always mounting upward around you, but you never succeed in plumbing its depths."

Having stopped in front of another shop, he saw a tailor standing outside with his hands folded and said to him, "Master Tailor, you are undoubtedly on the road to salvation."

"How do you make that out?"

"How do I make it out?" replied Glasscase. "I make it out from this, that inasmuch as you have nothing to do, you have no occasion for lying. The tailor," he went on, "who does not lie and sew flattery into his garments is out of luck. It is a very strange thing, but among all those who follow this trade you almost never find a workman who will give you a just fit though there are plenty who will give you a sinful one."

With regard to cobblers, he remarked that in their own opinion they never turned out a bad pair of shoes; for if the shoes were too tight and pinched the foot, that was the way they were supposed to be, as men of fashion preferred tight-fitting ones—all you had to do was wear them a couple of hours and they would be as comfortable as sandals; but if on the other hand they were too wide, that was all the better for the gout.

One young fellow with a keen mind, a clerk in the provincial court, pressed the licentiate with many questions and also brought him news of what was happening in the town, for Glasscase was in the habit of discoursing on every subject and responding to all inquiries that were put to him.

"Last night," the youth informed him, "a money-changer [36] who had been condemned to hang died in the jail."

"He did well in dying before the executioner had a chance to sit upon him."

In the San Francisco walk there was a group of Genoese, and as the licentiate went by, one of them called to him, saying, "Come over here, Señor Glasscase, and tell us a story." [37]

"No," was the answer, "I don't care to do so; I'm afraid you will take my million [37] back to Genoa with you."

On another occasion he met the wife of a shopkeeper with a very ugly daughter in front of her who was laden down with pearls and other trinkets. "That is a good idea," he said to the mother, "paving her like that; it makes walking easier for you."

Regarding pastry cooks, he observed that for many years they had been playing at *dobladilla* [38] but without paying the penalty, for they had raised the price of their wares from two to four, from four to eight, and from eight to half a real, at their own good will and pleasure.

He also had no end of fault to find with the puppet masters, saying that they were a lot of vagabonds who were guilty of indecency in the portrayal of sacred things; the puppets they employed in their shows made a mockery of devotion, and they sometimes stuffed into a bag all or nearly all the personages of the Old and New Testament, and then would sit down upon them to eat and drink in the alehouses and taverns. In short, it was a wonder that perpetual silence was not imposed upon them, or that they were not banished from the realm.[39]

When an actor dressed like a prince went by, Glasscase looked at him and said, "I remember having seen that fellow in the theater; his face was smeared with flour and he was wearing a shepherd's coat turned inside out; but at every step he takes off the stage, you would swear upon your word of honor that he was a gentleman."

"That may very well be," someone reminded him, "for there are many actors who are well born and sons of somebody." [40]

"That is true enough," replied Glasscase, "but what the stage stands least in need of is individuals of gentle birth. Leading men, yes, who are well mannered and know how to talk, that is another matter. For it might be said of actors that they earn their bread by the sweat of their brows, with an unbearable amount of labor, having constantly to memorize long passages, and having to wander from town to town and from one inn to another like gypsies, losing sleep in order to amuse others, since their own well-being lies in pleasing their public. Moreover, in their business, they deceive no one, inasmuch as their merchandise is displayed in the public square, where all may see and judge of it.

"Authors, too, have an incredible amount of work to perform and a heavy burden of care; they have to earn much in order that by the end of the year they may not be so far in debt that they will have to go into bankruptcy; yet for all of that, they are as necessary to the state as are shady groves, public walks and parks, and other things that provide decent recreation."

He went on to cite the opinion of a friend of his to the effect that a servant to an actress was a servant to many ladies at one and the same time: to a queen, a nymph, a goddess, a kitchen wench, a shepherd lass, and many times a page or a lackey as well, since the actress was used to impersonating all these and many other characters.

They asked him who was the happiest man that ever lived, and his reply was, "Nemo, for *Nemo novit patrem; Nemo sine crimine vivit; Nemo sua sorte contentus; Nemo ascendit in coelum.*" [41]

Of fencing experts he remarked that they were masters of a science or art which when they needed it they did not know how to employ, adding that there was something presumptuous in their seeking to reduce to infallible mathematical formulas the angry thoughts and impulses of their adversaries. But his special enmity was reserved for those who dyed their beards. He once saw two men engaged in a quarrel, the one being a Portuguese, the other a Castilian. "By this beard that I have on my face!" the Portuguese exclaimed, laying hold of his beard. It was at that point that Glasscase intervened. "Look here, man," he said, "don't say 'this beard that I *have* on my face'; what you mean is 'this beard that I *dye* on my face.'" [42] Another had a beard that was streaked with many colors, and the licentiate told him that it resembled an eggcolored dung heap. Still another had one that was half black and half white, the result of carelessness in letting the roots grow out, and he was warned by Glasscase not to be stubborn and get into an argument with anyone, or he was likely to be told that he lied by half a beard.[43]

He had a story to tell of a young woman who was very discreet and intelligent and who, by way of yielding to her parents' wishes, had consented to marry a graybeard. The night before the wedding day the groom went, not down to the river Jordan as the old wives say,[44] but to the bottle of aqua fortis and silver,[45] with which he proceeded to renovate his beard, turning it from snow-white to pitch black. When the hour appointed for the marriage ceremony arrived, the bride, judging the card by its spots,[46] insisted that her parents give her the husband they had promised, as she would have no other. They assured her that the man before her was the same one whom they had introduced as her betrothed. She maintained that he was not and brought witnesses to prove that the bridegroom whom her parents had promised her was white-haired and of grave aspect, and since this one did not answer that description, he must be some other and she was being tricked. Nothing could induce her to change her mind, and so the one with the dyed beard went away and the marriage was called off.

He had the same sort of grudge against duennas, and it was worth hearing what he had to say about the oaths they took and their faithlessness, their shroudlike headdresses, their prudery and their simperings, and their extraordinary miserliness. He found fault with them for their attacks of stomach weakness, their swooning, their way of talking with more falderals to their speech than they had on their bonnets—in short, their general uselessness and their affectations.

"How comes it, Señor Licentiate," someone said to him, "I have heard you speak ill of so many professions, but I have yet to hear you say anything about scriveners, although there is so much to be said?"

"I may be made of glass," he replied, "but I am not so fragile as to let myself drift with the current of public opinion, which most of the time is wrong. As I see it, the scriveners provide a grammar for backbiters, and are what the musical scale is to a singer; for just as one can go on to the other sciences only through the gate of grammar, and just as a musician must first hum [47] before he sings, so it is by speaking ill of scriveners, bailiffs, and other agents of the law that slanderers begin to display the malignity of their tongues. If it were not for the scrivener, truth would go through the world under cover, persecuted and mistreated, just as Ecclesiasticus says: '*In manu Dei potestas hominis est, et super faciem scribae imponet honorem.*' [48]

"The scrivener is a public official, and without his aid the judge cannot properly fulfill the duties of his office. Scriveners must be freeborn, neither slaves nor the sons of slaves, of legitimate birth and not bastards, nor should they come of any bad racial stock; they have to swear secrecy and loyalty and promise not to engage in any usurious practices; and neither friendship nor enmity, profit nor gain, should cause them to fail to fulfill their functions with a good and Christian conscience. If this office, then, calls for so many good qualities, why should it be thought that, of the twenty thousand scriveners that there are in Spain, the devil reaps his own special harvest? I do not believe, nor should anyone believe, that this is true; for I may tell you that they are the most necessary class of people that are to be found in well-ordered states, and if they take too many rights, they also commit too many wrongs, and out of these two extremes it is possible to strike a happy medium that causes them to look sharp and watch their step."

As for bailiffs, he declared it was not strange if they had many enemies, since it was their business to arrest you, to remove your property from your house, or hold you under guard while they ate at your expense. But he charged lawyers and solicitors with being negligent and ignorant, comparing them to doctors who, whether or not the patient recovers, collect their fee; these gentlemen of the legal profession did the same regardless of whether they won or lost their case.

Someone asked him which was the best land, and he replied that it was the one that was the most fertile and productive.

"I did not ask you that; what I meant was, which is the better region, Valladolid or Madrid?"

"Madrid for the extremes, Valladolid for the middle."

"I do not understand what you mean," said the one who had asked the question.

"In Madrid, the sky and earth; in Valladolid, the mezzanines." [49]

Hearing one man tell another that as soon as he had come to Valladolid his wife had fallen very ill, as the region [*tierra*] did not agree with her, Glasscase spoke up and said, "It would have been better for her if she had eaten earth [*tierra*] in case she is of a jealous disposition." [50]

Speaking of musicians and foot couriers, he implied that neither had much of a future, for the most that the latter could hope for was to become mounted couriers, while the former could look forward only to a place in the royal band. He likewise had something to say of those ladies known as courtesans [*cortesanas*], remarking that all or most of them were more courteous [*corteses*] than they were healthy [*sanas*]. In church one day he saw them bringing in an old man for burial, baptizing an infant, and conferring the bridal veil upon a woman, all at one and the same time, and he observed that religious edifices were battlefields where the old met their end, children conquered, and women triumphed.

When a wasp stung him on the back of the neck he did not dare shake it off for fear of breaking himself, but nonetheless he complained of it, and when asked how it was that he felt the wasp since his body was made of glass, he replied that the insect must be some slanderer, for their tongues and stings were sufficient to destroy bodies of bronze, not to speak of those made of glass.

A very fat friar happened to pass the place where he was standing. "That good father," said one of the listeners, "is so consumptive he can hardly walk." Glasscase was annoyed by this. "Let no one," he admonished them, "forget what the Holy Spirit has said: '*Nolite tangere Christos meos*' ";[51] and then, his anger increasing, he told them to look into the matter and they would find that of the many saints canonized by the church in those parts during the last few years and elevated to the number of the blessed, none had been named Captain So-and-So, or Secretary Don So-and-So to So-and-So, or the Count, Marquis, or Duke of This-or-That, but had been plain Friar Diego, Friar Jacinto, Friar Raimundo, etc. They had all been monks and friars, for religious orders are the orange groves of Heaven and provide the everyday fruit for God's table. He went on to say that the tongues of slanderers were like the eagle's feathers which gnaw and eat away all those of other birds that are placed with them.[52]

Concerning gamblers and gambling-house keepers he had extraordinary things to relate, averring that they were nothing but public cheats who would force the winner to contribute to the kitty, all the while hoping he would lose so that his opponent would obtain the deal and win and the house would get what was coming to it. He lauded the patience of one gambler who, despite the fact that he had been playing all night and losing and was in a hellish temper, nevertheless did not open his mouth but was willing to endure the martyrdom of a Barabbas, providing only that his opponent did not cut the cards. He also praised the conscientiousness of the keepers of certain respectable houses who would not think of permitting beneath their roof any games other than ombre and hundred-points, and yet, without any fear of complaints on the part of their customers, managed to come out at the end of the month with a larger kitty than those who permitted other games in which money changed hands in the twinkling of an eye.[53]

The short of the matter is, he said such things that, if it had

not been for the screams he gave when anyone touched or drew
near him, the garb that he wore, the limitations of his diet and the
manner in which he drank, his refusal to sleep anywhere except
under the open sky in summer and amid the straw in winter,
all of which obvious signs of madness have been set forth above,
no one would have believed that he was anything other than one
of the sanest individuals in this world. His illness continued for two
years or a little longer, and then a monk of the order of St. Jerome,
who was particularly skilled in teaching deaf mutes to understand
what was said to them and, to a certain degree, to talk, and who
had also had experience in curing the mad, undertook to treat the
Licentiate Glasscase, being moved to do so out of charity; and
treat him he did, and cured him, and restored him to his former
state of reason, sound judgment, and good sense.

As soon as he saw that his patient was once more a healthy man,
he clad him in scholastic garments and had him return to the capital, where Glasscase gave as many proofs of being sane as he formerly had of being mad, and where he was in a position to resume
his profession and render himself famous by it. The licentiate now
called himself Rueda [54] and not Rodaja, and he had no sooner
entered the city than he was recognized by the small boys, who,
seeing him dressed so differently than was his wont, did not dare
to shout at him or ask him any questions but merely followed him,
saying to one another, "This cannot be the madman Glasscase,
can it?" "My word, but it is. He is sane again; and yet one can be
a well-dressed madman. Let us ask him something and settle the
matter."

The licentiate heard all this and was silent, for he was more
abashed and bewildered now that he had his senses back than
he had been before. The word spread from the boys to the

grownups, and before Rueda had reached the place where the Councils were held, more than two hundred persons of every sort were following him. In the crowd was more than one professor, and upon reaching the court they all crowded around him; whereupon, becoming aware of the throng, he raised his voice and addressed them.

"Gentlemen, I am indeed the Licentiate Glasscase, but not the one you knew of old; I am now the Licentiate Rueda. Events and misfortunes such as happen in this world with Heaven's permission had deprived me of my reason, but God in His mercy has restored it to me. In view of the things I said to you when I was mad, you may form an idea of what I shall say and do now that I am sane. I am a graduate in law at Salamanca, where I studied under the handicap of poverty yet obtained second honors, from which you may infer that it was my own abilities rather than any favors shown me that won me the rank I hold. I have come here to this great sea that is the capital to swim and earn my living, but unless you leave me alone, I shall have come only to drown and meet my death. For the love of God, do not let your following me about become a persecution,[55] else that which I gained as a madman, namely, my livelihood, shall be lost through my having recovered my senses. Those questions that you used to ask of me in the public squares you may now put to me at home. They tell me that I used to answer them very well on the spur of the moment; but you shall see now how much better are the answers that I give when I have thought them over."

They all listened to him, and some of them drifted away. He returned to his lodgings with less of a crowd at his heels, but when he came out the next day, it was the same story all over again. He preached another sermon, but it did no good. It was

costing him much, and he was earning nothing by it, and when he saw that he was on the verge of starvation, he made up his mind to leave the capital and return to Flanders, where he thought to avail himself of the strength of his arm, since he could not make use of that of his intellect. Putting his resolution into effect, he exclaimed as he was about to take his departure, "O court, you who more than fulfill the hopes of audacious pretenders and cut short those of the competent, you provide in abundance for shameless mountebanks and let the wise who have a sense of shame die of hunger!"

Saying this, he set off for Flanders, where the immortality that he had begun to win in the domain of letters was achieved by him through force of arms, in the company of his good friend, Captain Valdivia, and even as he died he left behind him the reputation of being a prudent and very brave soldier.

THE COLLOQUY
OF THE DOGS

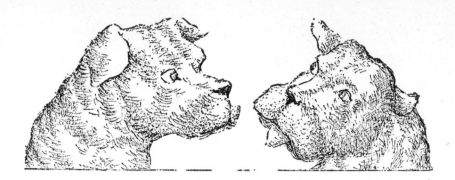

The Colloquy of the Dogs

Dialogue that took place between Cipión and Berganza, dogs belonging to the Hospital of the Resurrection, which is in the city of Valladolid, outside the Puerta del Campo, the said dogs being commonly known as those of Mahudes.[1]

CIPIÓN: Friend Berganza, let us leave our watch over the hospital for tonight and retire to this secluded spot, and here upon these mats, without fear of being overheard, let us enjoy that favor which Heaven has seen fit to bestow on both of us at one and the same time.

BERGANZA: Brother Cipión, I hear you speaking, and know that I am speaking to you, and yet I cannot believe it, for the reason that it seems to me something beyond the bounds of nature.

CIPIÓN: That is the truth, Berganza, and the miracle is all the greater in that we not only are speaking but are doing so in a coherent fashion, just as if we were capable of reason, whereas the difference between brutes and men lies in the fact that man is a rational animal and the brute an irrational one.

BERGANZA: I understand everything that you say, Cipión, and the fact that you say it and I understand it is fresh cause for wonderment. It is true that in the course of my life I have on many and divers occasions heard it said that we dogs possess great endowments, so great, indeed, that some have beheld in us a natural instinct so keen and lively as almost to lead to the belief that we have some little bit of understanding and are capable of thought.

CIPIÓN: What I have heard praised and stressed is our remarkable memory, our gratitude, and our great loyalty, which has led to our being depicted as the symbol of friendship. If you think about it, you must have seen upon those alabaster tombs, where the figures of the ones who are buried there are engraved, the image of a dog at the feet of husband and wife to signify that the married pair in their lives preserved toward each other an inviolable friendship and fidelity.

BERGANZA: I am well aware that there have been dogs so affectionate as to throw themselves into the same grave with the bodies of their masters, while others have refused to leave the spot and, taking no food, have ended their own lives there. I know also that next to the elephant the dog holds first place in the matter of seeming intelligence, and after him comes the horse, and lastly the monkey.

CIPIÓN: That is the truth; but you will have to admit that you have never seen or heard tell of any elephant, dog, horse, or ape that actually has spoken, which leads me to conclude that our being thus suddenly endowed with speech is one of those things that are known as portents, boding forth some great calamity that threatens the people, as experience has shown.

BERGANZA: In that case, I can almost believe it was a portent that I heard one time from a student when I was passing through Alcalá de Hernares.[2]

CIPIÓN: What was it you heard?

BERGANZA: I heard him say that there were five thousand students at the University that year and that two thousand of them were studying medicine.

CIPIÓN: Well, and what do you infer from that?

BERGANZA: What I infer is that those two thousand doctors must have patients to cure, in which case it would be a plague and a very great misfortune, or else they are going to die of hunger. But however that may be, here we are talking to each other. As to whether or not it is a portent or what it may be that Heaven has ordained, that is something that no human diligence or wisdom can foresee or prevent; and so there is no use in our discussing how it is or why we come to have the power of speech. It would be better for us, this fine day or fine night, to make ourselves at home here on these comfortable mats and, since we do not know how long it will last, take advantage of our good fortune by talking all night, without permitting sleep to interfere with this pleasure, which is one that I have long desired.

CIPIÓN: I too—ever since I had the strength to gnaw a bone I have wanted to talk in order to speak of those things that for so long have lain moldering or half forgotten in my memory.

BERGANZA: Now that I find myself so unexpectedly enriched with this divine gift of speech, I wish to enjoy and take advantage of it all I can, being in haste to tell everything that I can remember, even though it be confusedly and helter-skelter, since I do not know how soon I may be called upon to return this blessing that is but a loan.

CIPIÓN: Let us, then, friend Berganza, arrange it in this manner: tonight you will tell me the story of your life and all the troubles that you have been through up to now, and tomorrow, if we find that we still can speak, I will tell you mine; for it will be better to spend the time this way than in seeking to learn about the lives of others.

BERGANZA: Cipión, I have always looked upon you as a wise friend, and now more than ever, seeing that as a friend you wish to tell me your life story and listen to my own, while you have shown your wisdom by the manner in which you have apportioned the time allotted to the telling. But first have a look and see if anyone can hear us.

CIPIÓN: There is no one, I think, although there is a soldier nearby, but at this hour he is more likely to be asleep than to be eavesdropping on someone.

BERGANZA: In that case, seeing that I may speak freely, hear what I have to say, and if it tires you, either reprove me or tell me to be silent.

CIPIÓN: Go ahead and talk until dawn, or until we are in danger of being overheard, and I shall be glad to listen to you without interrupting any more than necessary.

BERGANZA: If my memory is correct, I first saw the light in the Slaughter House of Seville, which is just outside the Cattle Gate, and if it were not for what I am about to tell you, this would lead me to think that my parents must have been mastiffs reared by those troublemakers known as butchers. The first master I had was one Nicolás the Snubnose, a sturdy, thick-set, hot-tempered lad, as are all those who follow the butcher's trade. He taught me and the other young whelps, in the company of the aged mastiffs, to chase the bulls and seize them by the ears, and I soon became an expert at this.[3]

CIPIÓN: I do not wonder at it, Berganza, since evil doing comes from a natural predisposition and is an easy thing to learn.

BERGANZA: How am I to describe to you, brother Cipión, what I saw in that Slaughter House and the extraordinary things that went on there? First of all, you must know that all who work in that place, from the lowest to the highest, are individuals without soul or conscience and have no fear of the King and his justice. Most of them live in concubinage and are in reality carnivorous birds of prey who support themselves and their women friends out of what they steal. Every day on which flesh is eaten,[4] before it is daylight, a large number of young fellows and their wenches appear at the Slaughter House, all of them with baskets that are empty when they come but which when they leave are filled with choice cuts of meat, the servant maids carrying off whole lamb cutlets and loins.[5]

There is not a head of cattle killed but these people get their tithe, in the form of the best and most savory portions. Since in Seville there is no official contractor in charge of the meat supply, each one is free to take what he likes, the first animals slain being either the best or the ones that bring the lowest price; and with this arrangement, there is always an abundance for all. The owners have no choice but to trust these people—not to refrain from stealing, for that is out of the question, but to observe some moderation in the slices that they pilfer from the dead beasts, which they are in the habit of lopping and pruning as they would willow trees or grapevines.

Nothing, however, caused me more astonishment or made a

worse impression upon me than the butchers themselves, who would kill a man as quickly as they would a cow; falling out over nothing at all, they would just as soon stick one of their yellow-handled knives into a person's belly as fell a bull. It was a wonder if a day passed without quarrels and wounds and sometimes murders as well. They all prided themselves on being bullies and ruffians, and there was none of them who did not have his guardian angel in San Francisco Square, and before it he would lay propitiatory offerings in the form of loins and beef tongues. I heard one witty man remark that there were three places in Seville which the King had yet to bring under his jurisdiction: the calle de la Caza, the Costanilla, and the Matadero.[6]

CIPIÓN: If you are always going to spend as much time as this, friend Berganza, in describing the dispositions of the various masters you have had and the faults to be found with their occupations, we shall have to pray Heaven to grant us the gift of speech for at least a year, and even then, at the rate you are going, I am afraid you will not have finished with half your story. There is one thing of which I should like to advise you, and you will see the truth of it when I come to narrate the events of my own life: some stories are charming in themselves, while in the case of others everything depends on the way in which they are told. By this I mean to say that there are some that give us pleasure when told without preamble or verbal ornaments of any sort; and there are others that have to be dressed out in words and set off with facial expressions, gestures, and inflections of the voice, in which manner something is made out of trifles and pale and flabby narratives take on point and give pleasure. Please do not forget this advice, and see that you make good use of it from now on.

BERGANZA: That I will, if it is possible for me to resist the great temptation I feel to speak, which I can barely control.

CIPIÓN: Look well to your tongue; from it come the major ills of human life.

BERGANZA: I may tell you, then, that my master taught me to carry a basket in my mouth and to defend it against anyone who tried to take it away from me. He also pointed out to me the house where his woman friend lived, so that her maid would not have to come to the Slaughter House and I could take her every morning what he had stolen the night before. One day, in the early hours of the dawn, I was carrying her portion to her when I heard someone call me by name from a window. Looking up, I saw it was a very beautiful girl. I paused for a moment, and she ran down to the street door and called to me again. I went up to her to see what she wanted, and she, taking what I had in my basket, dropped an old shoe into it, whereupon I said to myself, "Flesh to the flesh."

"Run along, Gavilán, or whatever your name is," she said, "and tell your Master, Nicolás the Snubnose, not to put his trust in animals but to remember the old saying about 'a hair of the wolf'; and that goes for the basket." [7]

I could very well have taken the meat away from her, but I did not care to put my dirty butcher's mouth on those fair white hands.

CIPIÓN: You did quite right, for it is beauty's prerogative to be respected always.

BERGANZA: Having done that, I returned to my master without the meat and with the old shoe in place of it. He was surprised to see me back so soon, and upon catching sight of the clog he

knew at once that a joke had been played on him. At once he
took out his knife and struck at me so hard that if I had not leaped
to one side you would not now be hearing this story, nor many
others that I have in mind to tell you. I then took to my feet and
the road and made off across the fields back of San Bernardo, not
knowing where my luck might lead me.

That night I slept in the open, and the next day, as fate would
have it, I came upon a flock of sheep. As soon as I laid eyes on it,
I felt that my troubles were over, for guarding sheep appeared
to me to be a proper and natural employment for dogs, a most
virtuous occupation, comparable to that of the proud and mighty
who protect the humble and the weak. There were three shepherds there, and the moment he saw me one of them called out
"*To, to, to, to.*" [8] As I could ask nothing better than this, I went
over to him, lowering my head and wagging my tail. He ran his
hand along my back, opened my mouth and spit on it,[9] looked at
my teeth to see how old I was, and then told his companions that I
had every mark of good breeding.

At that moment the owner of the flock came up. He was
mounted on a gray mare, his saddle being one of the kind with
high trees and short stirrups,[10] and he carried a lance and a buckler,
which gave him the appearance of a coast guard rather than a
sheep raiser.

"Whose dog is this?" he asked. "It looks like a good one."

"Your Grace is quite right about that," replied the shepherd,
"for I have examined him well and his markings are of the best.
He just now came, and I cannot tell you where he belongs, but it
is not to any of the flocks around here."

"Very well then," said the owner, "put a collar on him—the
one that belonged to Leoncillo, the dog that died—give him the

same rations you do the others, and treat him well so that he will take a liking to the flock and stay with it."

With this he went away, and the shepherd put a steel-pointed collar on me, having first fed me, in a small trough, a large quantity of bread crumbs soaked in milk. At the same time he gave me a name, that of Barcino,[11] and I was quite content with my new master and my new job. I was very careful and diligent in guarding the flock, never leaving it except for my siesta, which I spent in the shade of some tree, some bank or cliff, or in a wood on the edge of one of the many brooks that flowed there. These hours of rest were not idle ones, for I spent the time in recalling many things, especially those that had to do with the life I had led in the Slaughter House; I thought of my master and all the others like him, and how subject they were to the whims of their mistresses. Oh, what things I could tell you of the many I learned in the school of that butcher-woman, my master's lady! But I shall say nothing about them, lest you take me for a long-winded gossip.

CIPIÓN: I have heard that a great poet among the ancients once remarked how difficult it was to keep from writing satires.[12] I shall not mind your gossiping a bit, providing you show that you belong to the brotherhood of light, not that of blood.[13] By this I mean to say that when you let fly your darts you should not wound or ridicule anyone; for even though it makes many laugh, gossip is not a good thing when it is deadly in effect, and if you can give pleasure without resort to backbiting, I shall look upon you as very wise.

BERGANZA: I mean to take your advice, and I look forward eagerly to the time when you will tell me what has happened to you; for seeing that you have been able to discover and correct my own faults so well, I expect to find both instruction and entertainment in the account you have to give me. But to take up the broken thread of my story— In the silence and solitude of the siesta hour it occurred to me that all I had heard concerning the life that shepherds lead surely could not be true if one was to judge from those that my master's lady read about in books when I went to her house. All those books had to do with shepherds and shepherds' lasses, who spent all their lives in singing and in playing on flageolets, rustic flutes, rebecs, reed pipes, and other strange instruments.

I used to stop to listen to her as she read how the shepherd of Anfriso sang so divinely in praise of the peerless Belisarda,[14] until in all the woods of Arcadia there was not a tree beneath which he had not sat to raise his voice in song from the moment the Sun left the arms of Aurora until Apollo had thrown himself into those of Thetis; and even after night had drawn its black curtain over the face of the earth, the swain's well-modulated and tearful laments were still to be heard. Then there was the shepherd Elicio, more amorous than bold, of whom it was said that, without attending to his own loves or his flock, he took upon himself the cares of others.[15]

There was also Fílida's great shepherd, unique painter of a single portrait, who had been more trusting than happy.[16] There were the troubles of Sireno and Diana's remorse, and the book went on to tell how she gave thanks to God, and to the wise Felicia, who by means of enchanted water undid all that network of snares and lighted up that labyrinth of difficulties.[17] I remembered other books of the same sort that I had read, but they are not worthy of being recalled.

CIPIÓN: Heed my advice, Berganza; gossip a little if you like, leave your sting, and pass on, and may your intentions always be pure even though your tongue belies them.

BERGANZA: In such a case the tongue never stumbles until the intentions first have fallen. If, however, out of carelessness or malice, I should lapse into backbiting and someone should reprove me for it, I will give him the same answer that the stupid poet Mauleón, a member of the Academy of Imitators, gave to one who asked him what was the meaning of *"Deum de Deo"*; he replied, *"De donde diere."* [18]

CIPIÓN: That was the answer of a dunce; but if you are wise, or wish to be, you will never say anything for which you will have to apologize. Proceed.

BERGANZA: What I will say now is this: all these reflections and many more led me to note how different were the habits and conduct of my shepherds and all others of that stripe [19] from those of the shepherds I had heard about from books; for if my masters ever sang, their songs were not tuneful and well composed, but consisted of a "look sharp for the wolf, Juanica" [20] and other similar expressions, and this not to the sound of pipes, flutes, and rebecs, but to the music made by knocking one crook against another or by rattling small pieces of tile between their fingers; and their voices were not delicate, sonorous, and admirable but so hoarse that, either alone or in chorus, they appeared to be shrieking or grunting rather than singing.

The greater part of the day they spent in hunting fleas on their bodies or in mending their sandals; nor did I hear any of them mention such names as Amarilis, Fílida, Galatea, or Diana, while none of these swains was called Lisardo, Lauso, or Jacinto, or Riselo, but instead were all Antones, Domingos, Pablos, or Llorentes. This confirmed me in the belief, which I think others should share, that all those books, though well written, are full of things that have been dreamed up for the amusement of persons with nothing better to do, and there is not a word of truth in them; for if there had been, there surely would have been among these shepherds of mine some vestige of that happy life, those pleasant meadows, spacious groves, sacred mounts, lovely gardens, clear running brooks, and crystalline fountains, as well as of those decent, poetically avowed love affairs, with a shepherd swooning here and a shepherd lass over there, now to the sound of a flute and now to that of a flageolet.

CIPIÓN: That will do, Berganza; get back on the path and go on.

BERGANZA: I thank you for that, friend Cipión; for I was warming up to the subject to such an extent that, if you had not warned me, I'd not have stopped until I had given you enough to fill a book about these deceivers. But the time will come when I shall tell all in a better and more connected fashion than now.

CIPIÓN: Look down at your feet, Berganza, and do not be flattering yourself; [21] by which I mean to say, you should remember that you are an animal and lack reasoning powers. If for the moment you appear to be able to reason, that is, as we have agreed, a supernatural circumstance and one that has never before been heard of.

BERGANZA: That might be true if I were still in my former state of ignorance; but now that I remember something I should have told you at the beginning of our conversation, I not only do not marvel at the fact that I am talking but dread the time when I shall cease to talk.

CIPIÓN: Can you not tell me what it is you have remembered?

BERGANZA: It is a certain thing that happened to me in the

company of a great witch, a pupil of La Camacha of Montilla.[22]

CIPIÓN: I should prefer that you tell me about it before you go on with the story of your life.

BERGANZA: No, that I do not wish to do until the time comes. Be patient, and let me relate what happened in the proper order, since that way it will give you more pleasure, unless you do not mind hearing the middle before the beginning.

CIPIÓN: Be brief, and tell it in your own way.

BERGANZA: Well, I liked the job of guarding the flock well enough, for I reflected I was eating my bread in the sweat of my own labor, and consequently was free of idleness, that root and mother of all the vices; for if I took my ease by day, I did not sleep at night, as the wolves very frequently attacked the fold and the alarm would then be given. No sooner had the shepherds cried out, "The wolf, Barcino!" than I would at once run off in the direction they had pointed at the head of all the other dogs. I would run through the valleys, search the hillsides, penetrate the groves, leap over ravines, and dart across the roads, and the next morning would return to the fold panting and completely exhausted, my feet cut and bleeding from the branches, without having found any trace of the wolf. What I did find was a dead sheep or lamb that had been killed and half devoured, and I despaired at seeing of how little use all my care and diligence had been.

The owner of the flock would then come riding up, and the shepherds would go to meet him with the skin of the slain sheep, whereupon he would blame them for their negligence and order them to punish the dogs for being so lazy. This they did, the blows and curses raining upon us. One day, seeing myself punished in this fashion through no fault of my own, and perceiving that all

my care, swiftness of foot, and bravery were of no avail in catching the wolf, I made up my mind to adopt a different method: I
would not go out to look for him as I usually did, far from the
fold, but would stay close by, since that was the place to which
the wolf would certainly come for his prey.

Every week the alarm was sounded, and on one very dark
night I was able to catch sight of those wolves from which it was
impossible to guard the flock. Crouching behind a clump of trees,
I let the other dogs, my companions, go on past, and then it was
I saw two of the shepherds seize one of the best sheep of the lot
and kill it in such a manner that, the next morning, it looked like
the work of that executioner the wolf. I was horrified and did not
know what to do, as it dawned upon me that the wolves were
none other than the shepherds themselves, who were supposed to
protect their charges. They as usual informed their master of the
raid and gave him the hide and a part of the meat, reserving the
better portion for themselves.

Once more the owner scolded them, and again the dogs were
punished. There were no wolves, but the flock continued to
diminish in size, and though I should have liked to reveal the truth,
I was without the power of speech. All this filled me with wonderment and anguish. "God help me!" I said to myself. "Who can
do anything about this evil? Who is in a position to make it
known that the defenders are the offenders, that the sentinels
sleep, the watchman robs, and the guardians kill?"

CIPIÓN: You are quite right about that, Berganza. There is no
greater or more slippery thief than the domestic one, and those
who are too trusting are far more likely to die than those who are
wary. The only trouble is that it is impossible for people in this
world to get along together unless there is mutual trust and con-

fidence. But let the matter rest there, for we do not want to be preaching sermons. Go on.

BERGANZA: So I made up my mind to leave this place even though it appeared to be so good a one, and to find some other, where, if they did not reward me for my good deeds, they at least would not punish me. I accordingly returned to Seville and entered the service of a very rich merchant.

CIPIÓN: What method do you employ in finding a master? For with times the way they are, it is very difficult these days to come upon a good one. The lords of earth are very different from the Lord of Heaven. The former, before they take a servant, must investigate his pedigree, test his abilities, note his appearance, and even pry into his wardrobe; whereas, when it comes to entering God's service, the poorest is the richest and the humblest is the highest born, providing only he be disposed to serve Him with a pure heart, in which case he is at once entered in His book of wages, his reward being such as many of the great ones of earth do not even envisage in their fondest desires.

BERGANZA: All that is preaching, friend Cipión.

CIPIÓN: You are right, I will say no more.

BERGANZA: You asked me how I went about finding a master. As you well know, humility is the basis of all the virtues, which cannot exist without it. It smoothes over obstacles, overcomes difficulties, and always leads to a glorious end, making friends out of enemies, tempering the wrath of the choleric, and diminishing the arrogance of the haughty. It is the mother of modesty and the sister of temperance. In short, vice holds no trump card against it that is of any use, for gentleness and meekness blunt the darts of sin.

It is of this virtue I avail myself when I would enter any household, having first taken a good look to make sure that it is the kind of house that can afford to keep and maintain a large dog. I then station myself at the door, and when I see some stranger coming in, I bark at him, but when the master comes I lower my head and run up to him, wagging my tail and licking his boots. If they beat me, I put up with it and, with the same meekness as before, fawn upon the one who has given me the blows, and they finally come to accept me when they see my persistency and good behavior. In this manner I get them to let me stay in the house, I serve them well, and they become quite fond of me and do not drive me away—it is I who drive myself away, or rather run away, though sometimes I find a master in whose house I would still be if it were not for the bad luck that follows me.

CIPIÓN: That is the same way I do with my masters. One would think we were mind readers.

BERGANZA: We are alike in that respect, if I am not mistaken, but I shall have more to say on the subject in due time, as I have promised. For the present, listen to what happened to me after I left the flock at the mercy of those wicked men. As I told you, I came back to Seville, which is the shelter of the poor and the refuge of the outcast but which in its greatness includes both the lowly and the high of station. Going up to the door of a mansion where a certain merchant dwelt, I went through my usual performance and within a short while was accepted there. At first they kept me tied up behind the door during the day but let me run loose at night, and I was very watchful and diligent, barking at strangers and growling at those who were not well known. At night I did not sleep but made the rounds of the yard and ran up to the terraces, acting as a sentinel not only for my own house but also for the neighboring ones.

My master was so pleased with the service I gave him that he ordered them to treat me well, and they gave me a ration of bread and bones from the table along with the kitchen leftovers, for which I showed myself to be very grateful by running and leaping madly every time I caught sight of my master, especially when he had been away from home. As the result of these demonstrations of joy and all my leapings and friskings, he gave orders that I was to be allowed to be turned loose both day and night. As soon as I found myself free, I ran up to him and ran all around him in circles, without venturing to lay my paws upon him, however, for I remembered that fable of Aesop which tells how a certain ass was so big an ass as to give his master the same caresses that a favorite lapdog did, which only won for him a sound thrashing.

As I see it, this fable teaches us that the pleasantries and witticisms of some are not becoming in others. Let the jester scoff, let the mountebank juggle and do his turns, let the rogue bray and imitate the songs of birds and the various things that men and animals do—all these accomplishments are well enough for those of low estate, but the man of high position should not stoop to them, since, no matter how clever he may be, they are not suited to his reputation and honored name.

CIPIÓN: You have said enough, Berganza; all that is understood. Get on with your story.

BERGANZA: I only wish that all those for whom I am saying this understood me as well as you do. There is a certain virtuous instinct in me that gives me great pain when I see a gentleman turn himself into a coarse buffoon or hear him boast that he knows how to play the shell game [23] and can dance the chacona better than anybody else! One such gentleman of my acquaintance boasted that at the request of a sacristan he had cut out thirty-two paper flowers to be laid upon the black cloth of the tomb they erect on the altar at Eastertime.[24] He brought all his friends to see his handiwork and made as much fuss about it as if he had been showing them the enemy banners and spoils on the tombs of his ancestors.

But to return to my story. This merchant had two sons, one of whom was twelve years old, the other about fourteen. They both attended the grammar school kept by the Jesuits, and they went there in great pomp, attended by their tutor and by pages who carried their books and what they called their *vademecums*. As I saw them set out in such style, in hand litters if the day was fair and in a carriage if it rained, I could not but think of the simple manner in which their father went to the Exchange to transact his business, attended by only one servant, a black, and mounted sometimes upon a mule that was none too well caparisoned.

CIPIÓN: You should know, Berganza, that it is the custom and inclination of the merchants of Seville and those of other cities as well to display their wealth and social position not in their own persons but in those of their offspring, for they loom greater in the shadow of the latter than they do in their own. And if by any strange chance they think of something other than their deals and contracts, they are extremely modest in what they spend on themselves. Since ambition and wealth are dying to be seen, this impulse finds an outlet in the sons, whose fathers spend as much upon them as if these youths were the heirs of some prince—and, indeed, they do sometimes procure titles for them and place upon their bosoms the mark that so distinguishes people of importance from the common herd.

BERGANZA: It is ambition, yes, but a generous one that seeks to improve its own lot without harm to another.

CIPIÓN: Ambition is seldom or never realized without harming another.

BERGANZA: We have said that we were not going to indulge in any ill-natured talk.

CIPIÓN: Yes, but I am not saying anything to hurt anyone.

BERGANZA: That only confirms me in an opinion I have often heard expressed. Some spiteful gossip may just have ruined ten pedigrees and slandered twenty worthy people, but if he is reproved for it, he will reply that he has said nothing at all, or if he did say something he did not mean it, and if he had thought that anyone would be offended he would not have said it. Upon my word, Cipión, you have to be very wise and very much on your toes [25] if you want to keep up a conversation for a couple of hours without slandering someone. I myself am but a brute beast, and yet every three or four sentences I utter I find words swarming to my tongue as mosquitoes do to wine, and all of them slanderous and malicious.

And so I will repeat what I have said before, that wrongdoing and the speaking of evil are something that we inherit from our forebears and drink in with our mothers' milk. This is clearly to be seen from the fact that the infant is no sooner out of swaddling clothes than he lifts his hand and threatens to take vengeance on someone he thinks has injured him; and almost the first articulate word that he speaks is "whore," applied to his mother or to his nurse.[26]

CIPIÓN: That is the truth. I confess my error and ask you to pardon me as I have pardoned you so many times. Let us throw trifles into the sea, as small boys say,[27] and after this let us refrain from such talk. Go on with your story—you were speaking of the pomp displayed by the merchant's sons as they went to the school kept by the Society of Jesus.

BERGANZA: I commend myself to Him,[28] come what may; and although it is difficult for me to refrain from ill-natured gossip, I mean to make use of a remedy that, I am told, was employed by one who was very much addicted to cursing. He repented of his bad habit, and after that every time that he swore he gave himself a pinch on the arm or else kissed the earth as a punishment for his fault; but in spite of it all he kept on swearing. And so I, every time I fail to observe the precept you have given me and my own intention in the matter, will bite my tongue until it hurts to remind me of my offense and keep me from repeating it.

CIPIÓN: If you make use of such a remedy as that, you are going to be biting your tongue so often that it will be impossible for you to speak at all.

BERGANZA: At least I shall do my best, and may Heaven make up for my shortcomings. But to continue. My master's sons one day left a notebook lying in the courtyard where I happened to be, and since the butcher had taught me to carry his basket, I at once picked up the *vademecum* and ran after them, being determined not to let go of it until I reached the classroom. Everything turned out as I had hoped it would. When my young masters saw me coming with the notebook in my mouth, gently grasped by the cord that bound it, they sent a page to take it from me, but I would not give it up until I had entered the room, which made all the students laugh. The older lad then came up to me, and I, very politely as I thought, placed it in his hand and remained there at the door, seated on my haunches and staring hard at the teacher, who was standing at his desk, reading to the class.

There is something about virtue that affects even one who possesses so little of it as I do, and I could not but take great pleasure in beholding the loving care and industry with which the pious fathers taught those children, bending the tender young twigs so that they would not grow into crooked branches and training them in the direction of virtuous conduct, which was taught them along with the instruction in letters. I saw how gently they reproved them, how mercifully they punished them, how they inspired them with good examples, incited them with prizes, and prudently indulged them. I saw, too, how they painted for them the horrible ugliness of vice and the beauty of virtue, in order that the young ones might flee the former and love the latter, and thus attain the end for which they were created.

CIPIÓN: You have put it very well, Berganza; for I have heard it said of those saintly ones that in the matter of prudence there is not their like in all the world, while as guides and leaders along the heavenly path few can come up to them. They are mirrors in which are to be viewed human decency, Catholic doctrine, an extraordinary wisdom, and, lastly, a profound humility that is the basis upon which the entire edifice of a holy life is reared.

BERGANZA: You are quite right about all that; and I will go on with my story by telling you that my masters were very well pleased with my having brought them their *vademecum*, and wished me to do it all the time. I readily complied, and as a result I now led the life of a king, or an even better one, for I had nothing to do but play with the students and was so tame as to allow them to put their hands in my mouth, while the smaller ones climbed on my back. They would toss their caps or hats across the yard and I would faithfully retrieve them with signs of great delight. They fed me whatever they could and enjoyed watching me as

I cracked walnuts or hazelnuts like a monkey, letting the shells fall and eating the tender part. Just to try me out, they even brought me a kerchief full of salad, which I ate as if I had been a human being. It was wintertime, when rolls and butter are to be had in great abundance in Seville, and I was kept so well supplied that not a few Antonios [29] were pawned or sold so that I might have my lunch.

In short, I led the life of a student, without hunger and without the itch—and I can give it no higher praise than that. For if it were not that the itch and hunger are the student's constant companions,[30] there would be no life that is pleasanter or more enjoyable, since virtue and pleasure here go hand in hand, and the young find diversion even as they learn. It was a certain lady who was to snatch me from this calm and enviable state, a lady who in those parts is known as Propriety,[31] and when one complies with her reasons many others have to go by the board. It appeared to those gentlemen the teachers that the half-hour intermissions were spent by the students not in going over their lessons but in playing with me; and so my masters were told not to bring me to school any more.

They obeyed and took me home, returning me to my old station at the door; the old gentleman, unmindful of the favor he had granted me by allowing me to run loose day and night, once more had them put a chain around my neck, and my body lay upon a small mat that they had placed for me behind the door.

Ah, friend Cipión, if you only knew how painful it is for a poor unfortunate to recall the happy days gone by! [32] You see, it is like this: when your whole life is constantly flooded with wretchedness, either your troubles soon will end in death or else you will become so accustomed to bearing them that even when

they are at their worst you will find some relief in force of habit; but when, as the result of a calamitous fate, you are suddenly and unexpectedly deprived of a prosperous and happy existence and are compelled to endure your former state of woe, you then feel a pain so intense that if it does not put an end to your life it is only in order to keep you alive and torment you the more.

In any case, I had to go back to my dog's rations and the bones that were tossed me by a Negress, one of the household servants, and even these were stolen from me by the tiger-striped cats, which, being free and light on their feet, found it easy to snatch up anything that fell beyond the reach of my chain. Brother Cipión, may Heaven grant you the blessings you desire, but if it does not bore you too much, please let me philosophize a little; for if I fail to speak of the things that come to my mind at this moment, my story will be incomplete and will bear no fruit.

CIPIÓN: Beware, Berganza. That desire to philosophize which you say has come to you may be a temptation of the devil; for gossip has no better veil for covering and excusing its wicked character than by conveying the impression that the one who indulges in it, in everything he says, is merely citing philosophical maxims, slander being masked as reproof, while the revelation of the faults of others is termed praiseworthy zealousness. If you examine closely the life of any slanderer, you will find it filled with vices and insolent pretenses. So long as you are aware of all this, philosophize as much as you like.

BERGANZA: You may be sure, Cipión, that I am bound to offend in the matter of backbiting—that's understood. But to continue. Being idle all day long, and idleness being the mother of reflection, I began thinking of certain Latin phrases that I remembered out of the many that I had heard when I was with my masters at school; and since it seemed to me that my mind had been somewhat improved, I resolved (assuming that I was able to speak) to make use of those phrases when occasion offered, but not in the same way that certain ignorant persons do. There are some whose native language is Spanish but who in their conversations let fly every so often with a concise bit of Latin, by way of giving their listeners to understand that they are great Latin scholars, whereas the truth is they can scarcely decline a noun or conjugate a verb.

CIPIÓN: In my opinion they are not as bad as some of those who really do know Latin and who, in speaking to a shoemaker or a tailor, pour it out like water.

BERGANZA: From that we may infer that he who speaks Latin in front of those who do not know it is as much to blame as he who pretends to know it when he does not.

CIPIÓN: There is another thing of which I would remind you, and that is that a knowledge of Latin does not keep a man from being an ass.

BERGANZA: There is no doubt of it, as is plainly to be seen when one recalls that in the time of the Romans Latin was spoken by everybody as his mother tongue, yet there must have been some blockhead among them who was a fool for all of that.

CIPIÓN: To know when to keep still in Spanish and when to speak in Latin calls for discernment, brother Berganza.

BERGANZA: Right you are; for it is as easy to talk nonsense in Latin as it is in Spanish. I have met learned lawyers and ponderous grammarians, who, with their scraps [33] of Latin, were the greatest bores in the world, and that not once but many times.

CIPIÓN: But let us leave all this and hear your philosophizings.

BERGANZA: You have already heard them.

CIPIÓN: How is that?

BERGANZA: I mean what I had to say about the use of Latin and Spanish. I began and you finished it.

CIPIÓN: And do you call such talk as that philosophizing? Away with it! But go ahead, Berganza, go ahead and sanctify the cursed plague of backbiting by giving it any name you choose; it will only give us the name of cynics, which means grumblers or faultfinders. Let's have no more of it, upon your life. Be still, and go on with your story.

BERGANZA: How can I be still and go on with my story at the same time?

CIPIÓN: What I mean to say is that you should tell it in a straightforward manner, without tacking on so many appendages that it comes to look like an octopus.

BERGANZA: Appendages are not what they are called. Why don't you say tails? [34]

CIPIÓN: You are falling into the same error made by one who remarked that there was nothing wrong in calling things by their right names, just as if it would not have been better, assuming that it was necessary to speak of them, to do so by means of circumlocution such as would temper the lewd impression which such words make upon the ears of the listener. A decent way of speaking is an indication of decency on the part of speaker or writer.

BERGANZA: I believe you. But as I was saying, fortune having taken me away from my studies and from my peaceful and happy life at school and having tied me up once more behind the door, compelling me to suffer the Negress's miserliness where before I had enjoyed the students' generosity, she now decreed that I should be deprived of what peace and leisure still was left me. You may take my word for it, Cipión, misfortunes seek out the unfortunate, and they will find him even though he be hidden in the far corners of the earth.

This Negress of our household was in love with another of the servants, a black like herself, who slept in the vestibule between the street door and the inner one behind which I was tethered. They could meet only at night, and for this purpose they had either stolen the keys or had had duplicates made. Almost every night the Negress would come down and, having stopped my mouth with a piece of meat or cheese, would open the door for her lover. They then would proceed to have a good time together, aided by my silence, which was purchased at the cost of many things the woman had pilfered.

Her bribes weighed on my conscience occasionally, but I reflected that without them my flanks would soon be touching each other and I would be changed from a mastiff into a greyhound. However, my better instincts prevailed and I resolved to do my duty by my master, seeing that I drew my wages from him and ate his bread; and this is something that not only self-respecting dogs, who are supposed to be grateful for favors received, should do, but all servants as well.

CIPIÓN: That, Berganza, I am willing to let pass for philosophy, since it is based upon truth and sound reasoning; and so go on and do not be making a rope, not to say a tail, out of your story.

BERGANZA: Very well; but first I wish you would tell me if you can just what philosophy is, for though I use the word I do not know what it means; all I know is that it is something good.

CIPIÓN: I will explain it to you briefly. The term is composed of two Greek words, *"philos"* and *"sophia,"* the former meaning a lover while the latter signifies wisdom; and so philosophy and philosopher come to mean the love, or a lover, of wisdom.

BERGANZA: You know a lot, Cipión. Who in the devil taught you all those Greek words?

CIPIÓN: Really, Berganza, you are very simple-minded to make so much of it, for these are things that every schoolboy knows—and I might add that there are some who pretend to know Greek, just as they do Latin, when they are in reality ignorant of it.

BERGANZA: I agree with you on that, and I'd like to see them put those fellows into a press, the way the Portuguese do with the Negroes from Guinea, and squeeze the juice out of what they know to keep them from going around the world deceiving people by a display of their scraps of Greek and faulty Latin.

CIPIÓN: Now is the time, Berganza, for you to bite your tongue, and I will do the same, for all that we are doing is to find fault.

BERGANZA: That is all very well, but I am not obliged to follow the example of one Charondas of Thurium.[35] He had proclaimed a law that no one was to enter the council chamber of that city bearing arms, under pain of death; but he forgot this and, himself, made his appearance there one day with a sword at his side, and when they pointed this out to him and reminded him of the penalty he had decreed, he at once unsheathed the sword and ran it through his bosom, thus being the first to make and break the law and to be punished for it.

I was not laying down any law, however. All I did was promise that I would bite my tongue if I found myself speaking ill of anyone. But we are not as strict as the ancients were. Today a law is made and tomorrow it is broken, and perhaps that is the way it should be. One promises to correct his faults and the next moment falls into greater ones. It is one thing to praise self-discipline and another to practice it on oneself, for it is true that "it is a long way from saying to doing." Leave tongue-biting to the devil; I don't intend to bite mine or make a point of any such scruples here on this mat where there is no one to see me and praise my noble resolve!

CIPIÓN: According to that, Berganza, if you were a human being you would be a hypocrite, and everything you did would obviously be false, a mere pretense covered by the cloak of virtue so that others might praise you, for that is the way with all hypo-crites.

BERGANZA: I do not know what I should do in that case but I do know what I want to do now, and that is, to refrain from biting my tongue. I still have so many things to tell you that I do not see how I am ever going to be able to finish. I am afraid that when the sun comes up it will find us groping here in darkness, without being able to talk.

CIPIÓN: Heaven will do better by us than that. Get on with your story and do not leave the wagon road by indulging in di-gressions that have nothing to do with the subject in hand. In that way, no matter how long it may be, you will be through with it soon enough.

BERGANZA: Well then, having observed the insolent, thieving, and disgraceful conduct of the two Negroes, I made up my mind like a good servant to put a stop to it by any means in my power, and my powers went further than I expected and I was able to carry out my intention. I have told you how the Negress was in the habit of coming down to have a good time with her lover, trusting to the silence of meat, bread, or cheese that she tossed me to keep me quiet. Bribes can accomplish much, Cipión!

CIPIÓN: Indeed they can. But do not allow yourself to be diverted; proceed.

BERGANZA: I remember, when I was a student, hearing the teacher quote a Latin saying, one of those that they call adages. It went like this: *"Habet bobem in lingua."* [36]

CIPIÓN: Oh, you and your Latin! Have you already forgotten what we were saying a short while ago about those who mingle scraps of Latin in their conversation?

BERGANZA: But this Latin is right to the point. The Athenians among others made use of a piece of money with the figure of an ox on it; and whenever any judge failed to say or do that which was right and just, for the reason that he had been bribed, they would remark, "That one has the ox on his tongue."

CIPIÓN: The saying doesn't fit here.

BERGANZA: Why, isn't it clear enough that it was the Negress's bribes that kept me silent for so long so that I would not bark when she came down to meet her black paramour? That is what led me to say that bribes can accomplish much.

CIPIÓN: And I have agreed with you on that. If it were not that it would take too long, I could cite you a thousand examples that would prove the point, and I may do so, if Heaven but grant me the time, opportunity, and gift of speech to tell you my life story.

BERGANZA: May God fulfill your wish—but listen to me. My good intentions finally overcame the Negress's wicked bribes. As she came down one night for her accustomed pastime, I threw myself on her without barking, so as not to awaken the household, and in a second I had torn her chemise to bits and had taken a bite out of her thigh, a little jest on my part that was sufficient to keep her—and no joke about it—in bed for more than a week, pretending to her master and mistress that she was suffering from some illness or other. But she recovered and came back another night, and I once more fell upon my bitch [37] and, without biting her, scratched her body all over as if I had been combing a piece of wool. Our battles were silent ones, and I always came out the victor, the Negress being badly handled, while her feelings suffered still more. She had her revenge, however, in a manner that affected my health, for she deprived me of my customary rations and of bones until my own bones began showing through my skin so plainly that you could count the knobs on my spine.

Nevertheless, while they might take away my food, they could not stop me from barking. In order to put an end to me once and for all, the Negress then brought me a sponge fried in lard, but I saw through the trick, realizing that to eat this would be worse than eating poison mixed with pounded glass, since it would cause the stomach of the one that took it to swell up, and he would not be able to get rid of it until he was rid of life itself. Inasmuch as it seemed to me impossible to guard against the snares of such unworthy enemies, I decided to get out of their sight and run away. Finding myself off the leash one day, and saying nothing to God or anyone in the house, I dashed out into the street and had not gone a hundred paces when, as luck would have it, I met the constable of whom I told you at the beginning of my story, who was a great friend of my master Nicolás the Snubnose. He no sooner laid eyes on me than he recognized me and called me by name, and I also recognized him and went running up to him with my usual ceremonies and caresses.

"This," he said, taking me by the neck and speaking to his men, "is a famous watchdog that used to belong to a friend of mine. Let us take him home with us."

The idea suited the men well enough, who said that if I was a watchdog, I ought to be of use to them. They wanted to take me by force, but my new master told them that was not necessary as I knew him and would come of my own accord. I have forgotten to tell you that the collar with the steel points I wore when I ran away from the sheepfold was stolen from me by a gypsy in a tavern, and there in Seville I had none; the constable now gave me another one, made of brass. Pause and reflect, Cipión, how variable is the wheel of fortune: yesterday I was a student, and today, behold, I am assistant to a constable.

CIPIÓN: That is the way the world goes. There is no reason to dwell on the ups and downs of fortune, just as if there were any great difference in serving a butcher and serving a constable. I cannot patiently endure hearing some men complain of the way fortune has treated them when the most they could ever hope for out of life was to be stable boys. Yet how they curse and rail, simply so that the one who hears them may think that they have fallen from some lofty, prosperous, and happy state into their present lowly condition.

BERGANZA: You are right. This constable, I may explain, was a friend of a certain scrivener who accompanied him on his rounds, and the two of them were living with a couple of wenches of whom it cannot be said that they were more or less disreputable, for it was distinctly more in their case. True, they had rather pretty faces, but they were impudent creatures and full of whorish wiles, and they served as net and bait for a variety of fishing on dry land. They dressed in such a fashion that you could at once spot them for what they were and could see at the distance of a harquebus shot that they were ladies of a free and easy way of life.

They were always on the hunt for foreigners, and when fair time came at Cadiz or at Seville they reaped a veritable harvest, and there was not a single Breton [38] whom they did not victimize. When the unwashed fellow [39] fell in with these clean lasses, the latter would promptly notify the constable and the scrivener of the lodging house to which the pair were going, and the two men would then come upon them in the act and arrest them as fornicators. They never took them to jail, however, as the foreigners always bought them off.

It happened, then, that Colindres (for that was the name of the constable's girl friend) fished up a greasy Breton [40] and arranged with him to dine and spend the night at her lodgings. In the meantime she had tipped off her lover, and she and the stranger were no sooner undressed than we all descended upon them, the constable and his men, the scrivener, and I. The Breton made a great fuss, and, moved by sympathy, the scrivener finally let himself be persuaded to reduce the fine to a mere hundred reales.

The Breton then asked for a pair of wide leather breeches that he had left on a chair at the foot of the bed, for he wanted the money that was in them to pay for his liberty, but they were nowhere to be found. The reason was that as soon as I had entered the room my nostrils had been greeted by the pleasing smell of meat; following the scent, I had found a wonderful slice of ham in a pocket of those trousers, and in order to get at it and enjoy it without attracting attention I had dragged the trousers into the street, where I fell upon the ham with a right good will. When I returned to the room I heard the Breton screaming, in a bastard tongue I was barely able to understand, that someone had taken his breeches and he wanted them back as he had in them

"fifty *escuti d'oro in oro*." [41] The scrivener was under the impression that either Colindres or the constable's men had stolen
them, and the constable was of the same opinion. He called them
to one side and questioned them, but no one confessed, and there
was the very devil to pay.

When I saw what was happening I ran back into the street
where I had left the trousers, meaning to restore them to their
owner, since the money meant nothing to me; but they were no
longer there, for some lucky passer-by had made off with them.
When the constable saw that the Breton had no money for a
bribe, he was in despair and decided to get it out of the landlady.
He called to her, and she came down half clad; and when she saw
Colindres naked and weeping and perceived how angry the constable and the scrivener were, while the constable's men meanwhile were ransacking everything in the room, she was anything
but pleased. The constable thereupon told her to go and get some
clothes on and come along with him to jail on a charge of harbor-
ing in her house men and women of a disreputable way of life.
There was then more confusion than ever, with everyone screaming at the top of their voices. It was a perfect bedlam.

"Sir Constable," said the landlady, "and you, Sir Scrivener,
don't be playing any of your tricks on me, for I am wise to them
all. Don't try to bluff me with any big talk but in God's name
shut your mouths and get out of here. If you don't, faith and I'll
throw the shop out the window and show up the whole gang of
you! [42] I know Señora Colindres very well, and I also know that
for many months the constable has been her man. Don't force
me to say any more but give this gentleman back his money and
let us all be good friends. For I can tell you I'm a respectable
woman, I am, and my husband has a certificate of nobility with

a perpenan rei de memoria,[43] lead seals, and everything, God be praised! I run a decent house, I do, and treat everybody fair. My price list is tacked up on the wall there where everyone can see it, so don't start anything with me, or by God I'll finish it! I suppose I'm responsible if my guests bring in women! They have keys to their rooms, and I'm no sphinx [44] that I should be able to see through seven walls."

My masters were astounded as they listened to the landlady's tirade and heard her telling them the story of their lives; but inasmuch as there was no money to be had unless they got it out of her, they insisted that they must carry her off to jail. She called on Heaven to witness the injustice and injury they were doing her in the absence of her husband, and he a gentleman of such high standing. The Breton was bawling for his fifty crowns, while the constable's men sought to convince him that—God forbid!—they had not seen his breeches. The scrivener, meanwhile, suggested to the constable in a whisper that they ought to search Colindres, as he suspected she had the money, knowing as he did that she was in the habit of going through the pockets and hiding places of those who became involved with her. She on the other hand maintained that the Breton was drunk and must be lying about it.

In short, all was confusion, with everyone screaming and cursing at once, and there apparently was no way of settling the matter, nor would it have been settled if at that moment the lieutenant to the Chief of Police [45] had not entered the room. Happening to visit the lodging house, he had heard voices and had come to investigate. When he asked what the screaming was all about, the landlady told him in great detail. She told him who Colindres was (that young lady was dressed again by this time) and informed him of the notorious relationship that existed between her and the constable; speaking so loudly that she could be heard out in the street, she proceeded to dwell on the tricks they played and their method of robbing people, at the same time excusing herself by saying that no woman of ill fame had ever entered her house.

She made herself and her husband out to be saints and directed a maidservant to run and fetch a strongbox containing her husband's patent of nobility so that the Señor Lieutenant might have a look at it, remarking that he would be able to see for himself that the wife of so respectable a husband could not be guilty of any misdemeanor, for if she was reduced to keeping a rooming house it was through no fault of hers, since God knows she did not like the business and only wished she had a small income to assure her of her daily bread so that she might get out of it.

"Sister," said the lieutenant, who was bored by all this talk about nobility, "I am willing to believe that your husband is a gentleman, but you'll have to admit that he is a gentleman innkeeper."

"But a most honorable one," replied the landlady. "Is there any family in all the world that does not have some blot on its escutcheon?"

"What I would advise you to do, sister, is to get some clothes on, for you're coming along to jail."

At hearing this the landlady fainted and fell to the floor; they threw water on her, and she came to herself and began screaming. The lieutenant, however, was not to be swayed and carted them all off to prison, namely, the Breton, Colindres, and the landlady. As I afterward learned, the Breton not only lost his fifty crowns but had to pay an additional ten and costs. The landlady received the same fine, while Colindres went free. And the very day they freed her she fished up a sailor who paid what she had lost on the Breton, for the same trick was worked on him. From all of which you can see, Cipión, how great was the harm that resulted from my covetousness.

CIPIÓN: You had better say, from your master's villainy.

BERGANZA: Well, anyway, listen; for there is more to come, although it pains me to speak ill of constables and scriveners.

CIPIÓN: Yes, but speaking ill of one of them is not to speak ill of all of them; for there are very many good and faithful scriveners [46] who stay within the limits of the law and who like to do you a favor without harming a third party; they do not all drag out lawsuits or take fees from both sides, nor do they all charge more than is their right; not all of them go about prying into the lives of others for the sake of ensnaring people in the web of justice; they are not all in league with the judge with a "You shave me and I'll cut your hair" arrangement; nor are all bailiffs allied with vagabonds and cheats, and not all of them have women friends to work such tricks as your master did. There are many who are gentlemen by nature, with gentlemanly instincts; many who are not bold, insolent, ill bred, and underhanded, like those who go through taverns measuring the swords that foreigners carry and who, when they find a blade that is longer than the law allows, bring about the downfall of its owner. Not all of them arrest persons and free them at their pleasure and are judge and lawyer at one and the same time.

BERGANZA: My master aimed higher than that; he took another path. Priding himself on his bravery and the famous captures that he made, he contrived to keep up his reputation in this regard without danger to his person but at some cost to his purse. One day, at the Jerez Gate, he had an encounter with six notorious ruffians without my being able to give him any assistance

whatsoever, for I was muzzled—I wore the muzzle during the day
but at night he took it off. I was astonished at his fearlessness: he
dashed in and out between the swords wielded by his six opponents as if they had been so many willow boughs. It was a
marvelous thing to see his lightness of foot as he fell upon them
and to watch his thrusts and parries while all the time he kept one
eye out to make sure no one attacked him from the rear. In short,
I and all the others who watched the fight took him to be another Rodamonte. Having driven his enemies back all the way
from the Jerez Gate to the statues that stand in front of Master
Rodrigo's college,[47] a distance of more than a hundred paces, he
left them in custody there and returned to pick up the spoils of
battle, which amounted to three scabbards that the ruffians had
left behind them. He then went to show them to the Chief of
Police, who, if my memory serves me right, was the Licentiate
Sarmiento de Valladares,[48] noted for having wiped out the bandits of Sauceda.[49]

After that, people would stare at my master as he went down
the street and would point him out, saying, "There goes the
brave fellow who dared to fight the flower of Andalusian bad
men singlehanded." He spent all that day strolling through the
city to show himself off, and that night we went to a house in
Triana,[50] in a street near the Powder Mill. After he had taken
a peek (as they say in the song) to make sure that no one saw
him, my master entered the house and I followed him into a courtyard where all those who had participated in the fray were gathered. They were without cloaks or swords, and all of them had
unbuttoned their garments for greater comfort. One of them, who
must have been the host, held a large pitcher of wine in one hand
and in the other a huge tavern bumper, which he filled with a

choice and foaming vintage as he drank to the health of the company.

No sooner did they catch sight of my master than they all ran up to him with open arms. They all drank his health, and he returned the compliment. Indeed, he might have kept it up indefinitely for, being of an affable disposition, he did not like to offend anyone over trifles. I wish I could tell you all the things that took place there, the dinner they had, the fights and thefts they related, the way in which they commended or reproved their ladies and heaped praises on one another, their references to their absent comrades, their talk of swordsmanship and the manner in which they arose in the middle of the meal to indulge in mock skirmishes and show how the thing was done, and the strange words that they used. And lastly I should like to describe for you the appearance of their host, to whom they all looked up as their master and father. If, however, I were to undertake all this, I'd become involved in a labyrinth from which it would be hard to extricate myself.

To make a long story short, I learned for a fact that the keeper of the house, whose name was Monipodio, was a fence for thieves and a protector of ruffians and that the big fight in which my master had engaged had all been prearranged, it having been understood that his opponents were to retire and leave their scabbards, which he now paid for, together with the entire amount that Monipodio said the dinner had cost. The feasting kept up until dawn, to the great enjoyment of all present.

A little later someone informed the constable of a ruffian from abroad, a very dashing fellow, who had just come to town—he must have been braver than those gathered here, which was the reason for their informing on him. The following night my master captured him as the stranger was lying naked in bed, but I could tell from the man's build that if he had been clothed he would not have let himself be taken so easily.

As a result of this capture, following close upon the fight, my master's reputation for bravery grew, though he was in reality more cowardly than a rabbit, and it was only by such wining and dining that he was able to sustain it. In fact, all the income from his office along with what he got from his double dealing went for this purpose. But be patient and hear what happened afterward. I will tell you the truth about it, without adding or subtracting anything.

A couple of robbers in Antequera had stolen a very good horse and brought it to Seville, and in order to sell it without incurring any risk they hit upon a stratagem which to my mind was a wise and clever one. The two of them went to different lodging houses, and one of them then appeared in court to ask for a judgment against Pedro de Losada, who, he claimed, owed him four hundred reales on a loan, as evidence of which he presented a note bearing Losada's signature. The lieutenant ordered that the note be submitted to Losada to see if he would acknowledge it. The other thief admitted that the signature was his, and he was thereupon ordered to make good the amount or go to jail.

The task of putting this order into execution fell to my master and his friend the scrivener. They conducted one thief to the other's lodgings and after the signature and debt had been duly confirmed proceeded to attach the horse as security. My master no sooner saw the animal than he was greatly taken with him and made up his mind to have the mount for his own in case of a sale. When the time prescribed by law had passed without the debt's having been paid, the horse was placed on the auction block and was knocked down on the first bid for fifteen hundred reales, though he was worth half as much again, to a third party acting in my master's behalf. Thus one robber collected on a debt that was not due him, the other had a receipt for which he had no use, and my master was left with a steed that was to bring him worse luck than the Sejan horse did to its owners.[51]

The thieves promptly decamped, and two days later, after my master had repaired the horse's trappings and fitted it out in proper fashion, he made his appearance in San Francisco Square, more vain and pompous than a villager dressed for a feast day. He received innumerable congratulations on the fine purchase he had made, which, everyone assured him, was worth one hundred and fifty ducats if an egg was worth a maravedi; and so he continued prancing up and down as if he were taking part in a drama with the market place as a theater. But while he was putting his steed through its paces, two men of impressive appearance and very well clad came up to him.

"In God's name," cried one of them, "if that isn't Ironfoot, my horse that was stolen from me a short time ago at Antequera!"

The four servants who were with him asserted that this was the truth, that this was indeed Ironfoot, their master's stolen mount. My own master was taken aback, but the rightful owner went to court and produced his evidence, which was so good that the case was decided in his favor and the constable was dispossessed. The news then spread as to how the thieves had made a mockery of the law by using it to sell stolen property, and nearly everyone was glad that my master's avarice had at last burst the bag.[52]

His troubles did not stop there, however. The Chief of Police had received word that robbers were abroad in the San Julián quarter; and that very night, as he was passing a street intersection, he caught sight of a man running and, seizing me by the collar, sicked me on: "Get the thief, Gavilán! Get him, Gavilán! Get him!" Being tired of my master's evil-doings, I obeyed the Chief's order with a right good will and fell upon the runaway, who was my own master, and brought him to the ground without his being able to help himself; indeed, had they not with great difficulty pulled me off him, I'd have had my revenge three or four times over. The constable's men wanted to punish me and would have clubbed me to death, but the Chief would not permit it. "Let no one lay hands on him," he said, "for this dog was merely doing what I ordered him to do." Nevertheless, I knew they had it in for me and, without waiting to say good-by to anyone, I slipped through a hole in the wall and dashed across the field and by dawn was in Mairena, a town that is four leagues from Seville.[53]

My good luck would have it that I should there fall in with a company of soldiers who, I was told, were on their way to take ship at Cartagena. Among them were four ruffians, friends of my master, and the drummer had formerly been the constable's assistant; he was, moreover, a great buffoon, as most drummers are. They all recognized me and spoke to me and made inquiries concerning my master as if I had been able to reply to them; but the drummer was the one who took the greatest fancy to me, and so I decided to go with him if he would permit it and follow the troops wherever they went, even though it might be to Italy or Flanders. For it seems to me, and I trust you will agree with me, that while there is truth in the old proverb which says "He who is a fool at home will be a fool in Castile," travel in foreign lands and intercourse with various peoples is nevertheless the thing that makes men wise.

CIPIÓN: The truth of that is shown by a remark that a very intelligent master of mine once made. He said that the reason the famous Greek known as Ulysses was called the wise was, simply, that he had traveled far and wide and had come to know the people of various nations. I accordingly approve the resolution you formed to go wherever they might take you.

BERGANZA: Well then, I may tell you that this drummer, by way of adding to his stock of buffooneries, began teaching me how to dance to the sound of the drum and to perform other monkeyshines so foreign to our nature that no other dog would have been able to learn them, as you will perceive when I tell you of them. We marched by slow stages, there was no commissary over us, the captain was a mere lad but a fine gentleman and a great Christian, it was not long since the lieutenant had left the pages' hall at court, and the sergeant was a shrewd fellow and an old hand at conducting recruits to the point of embarkation. The company was full of rascally adventurers who, in the villages through which we passed, committed more than one outrage that resulted in curses being heaped on the head of one who did not deserve them. It is the misfortune of the good prince to be blamed by his subjects for the offenses that they commit against one another through no fault of his, since even though he sought to do so, he would not be able to remedy these wrongs, most of which are a part of the hardships, inconveniences, and severities that war brings with it.

The short of it is that in less than two weeks' time, with the good mind that I possess and as a result of the effort that my newly chosen master expended in teaching me, I learned to dance "for the King of France and not for the churlish tavernkeeper's wife." [54] He taught me to bound and leap like a Neapolitan horse and to go round and round like a mule at a millstone, along with other things which, if I had not observed a degree of moderation in showing off my accomplishments, would have led one to suspect that it was some demon in the form of a dog that was performing these tricks. They gave me the name of "the Wise Dog," and we would no sooner arrive at the place where we were to camp than my master would go through the town inviting one and all to come and view my marvelous abilities and accomplishments, at such and such a house or hospital, the price of admission varying from four to eight maravedis, depending upon the size of the village.

After such an announcement and all the praise bestowed upon me, there was no one who did not turn out to have a sight of me, and they all left full of wonderment and satisfied with what they had witnessed. My master made so much money by all this that he was able to support six of his comrades in a manner fit for kings; but avarice and envy awakened in the ruffians a desire to steal me, and they began looking for an occasion to do so, for there are many who are very fond of making their living by so easy a means as this. That is why it is there are so many puppeteers and pageant showmen in Spain, so many who go about selling rhymes and cheap jewelry, when their entire stock of trade, if they were to dispose of it, would not suffice to keep them a single day; yet you will find them in the alehouses and the taverns all the year around, which leads me to believe that they get the money for their drunkenness from some other source than the trades they are supposed to follow. They are all a lot of useless, good-for-nothing vagabonds, a lot of wine sponges and bread weevils.

CIPIÓN: Let's not go over all that again, Berganza! Continue, for the night is passing, and I should not like for us to be left in the shades of silence when the sun comes up.

BERGANZA: Say no more, but listen. You know how easy it is, when you have invented something, to keep adding to it. Seeing how well I was able to imitate the Neapolitan horse, my master had some embossed blankets made for me, and he also fashioned a little chair, which he fitted on my back, and on it he placed a tiny figure of a man with a lance in his hand as if engaged in the game of rings. He showed me how to run directly for a ring held between two posts; and on the day on which I was to do this, he went through the town announcing that I would perform this feat along with other new ones never before seen—which I made up out of my own noddle, as the saying goes, in order not to make him out to be a liar.

In the course of our march we came to Montilla, home of that great and famous Christian the Marquis of Priego, lord of the houses of Aguilar and Montilla. My master, at his own request, was billeted in a hospital; and he at once went through the town to make his usual proclamation. Inasmuch as the fame of "the Wise Dog" and his accomplishments had preceded us, in less than an hour the courtyard was filled with people. My master was delighted at the prospect of so good a harvest and on that particular day excelled himself as a showman.

The entertainment began with my leaping through the rim of a sieve which resembled a barrel hoop. He made the customary requests of me, and I performed my tricks. When he lowered a quince-tree bough that he held in his hand, that was the sign for me to jump; and when he raised it, I was to remain quiet. The first command that he gave me on that day—a memorable one among all the days of my life—was the following:

"Come, friend Gavilán, jump for that young-old man you know who souses his beard; or, if you don't want to jump for him, do it for the pomp and finery of my lady Pimpinel of Paphlagonia, companion to the servant wench of Valdeastillas.[55] Don't you like that order, Gavilán my boy? Then jump for the bachelor Passillas [56] who signs himself a licentiate though he has no degree. Oh, but you're lazy! Why don't you jump? But I'm on to your tricks. Come now, jump for the wine of Esquivias, famous as that of Ciudad Real, San Martín, and Rivadavia."

He lowered the bough and I leaped, being aware of the humor he was in and his malicious intentions. He then turned to the audience and addressed them in a loud voice. "Let not this worthy assemblage think," he said, "that this dog's accomplishments are any laughing matter. I have taught him some two dozen tricks, and to see the least of them the hawk would come flying; by which I mean to say, it's worth coming thirty leagues to see them. He can dance the saraband and the chacona better than the one who invented them; he can drink an azumbre of wine without spilling a drop; he can sing do-re-mi-fa like a sacristan—but all these things, and many others of which I have yet to tell you, your Graces will have a chance to see for yourselves during the time that the company is here. And now let's have our wise friend give one more jump and then we'll get down to business."

At this the audience, which he had termed an assemblage,[57] was in suspense, being eager to see all the tricks of which I was capable. "Come, Gavilán, my boy," my master now said to me, "with your usual nimbleness and cleverness repeat all the jumps you have made; but this time it is to be for the sake of the famous witch who, they tell me, lives in this town."

No sooner had he said this than the hospital matron, an old woman who looked to be more than seventy,[58] raised her voice and began screaming, "Villain, charlatan, swindler, son of a whore, there is no witch here! If it's Camacha[59] you mean, she has already paid for her sins and God knows where she is now; but if I am the one you're talking about, you clown, I am not and never have been a witch, and if I've had the reputation of being one, that is due to false witnesses and a disregard of the law on the part of a judge who was presumptuous and ill informed. Everyone knows the life of penance that I have led, not for the deeds of witchcraft which I did not commit but for my many other sins. And so, you rascally drummer, get out of this hospital, or I swear I'll put you out faster than you want to go." With this she began shrieking so loudly and continuously and heaped such a storm of abuse upon my master that he was utterly dumfounded. In short, it was quite out of the question for the show to go on.

He was not greatly concerned over the row, however, for he had the money in his pocket and on another day, in another hospital, could make up for anything he might have lost here. The people went away cursing the old woman, calling her a witch and a sorceress and a bearded old hag. But in spite of it all we stayed there that night, and thus it was I came to meet the old hag alone in the yard.

"Is that you, Montiel, my son?" she said to me. "Is it you, by any chance?"

I raised my head and stared at her long and hard, and when she saw this her eyes filled with tears and she came over to me and threw her arms about my neck. She would have kissed me on the mouth if I had let her, but I was nauseated at the thought and would not consent.

CIPIÓN: You did well; it is no treat but a torture to permit oneself to be kissed by an old woman.

BERGANZA: What I wish to tell you now ought to have been told at the beginning of my story, in which case we should not have been so astonished at finding ourselves with the gift of speech.

"Montiel, my son," the old woman went on, "follow me so that you will know where my room is, and tonight come to see me when we can be alone together. I will leave the door open." And she added, "I have many things to tell you concerning your life that will be to your advantage to know."

I dropped my head in token of obedience, and this, as she afterward informed me, convinced her that I was indeed the dog Montiel that was the object of her search. I was left astonished and bewildered as I waited for night to come, for I was anxious to find out what the upshot of this mystery or miracle of which the old woman had spoken would be. Having heard her called a witch, I expected great things of my meeting with her and what she might have to tell me.

At last I found myself closeted with her in her room, a small, dark, low-ceilinged one, lighted only by the feeble glow of an earthenware lamp. The old woman trimmed the lamp and then, seating herself upon a small chest, drew me to her and without saying a word began embracing me once more, while I took good care to see that she did not kiss me.

"I always hoped to Heaven," she began, "that before these eyes of mine should be closed in their last sleep I might have a sight of you, my son; and now that I have seen you, let death come and relieve me of this tired life of mine. You must know, my lad, that in this town there formerly lived the most famous witch in all the world. She was called Camacha of Montilla and was so outstanding at her trade that the Erichthos,⁶⁰ the Circes, and the Medeas, of whom I am told the storybooks are full, could not come up to her. She caused the clouds to congeal whenever she felt like doing so and with them covered the face of the sun, and when the whim seized her the most troubled sky would become serene once more. She would bring men back in an instant from far-off lands, and she had a marvelous cure for maidens who had been a bit careless in guarding their virginity.

"She took care of widows in such a way that they might be disrespectable and still be respected, she undid marriages, and married off those whom she pleased. She had fresh roses in her garden in December, and in January sowed wheat. As for growing watercress in a bowl, that was the least of the things she did, and it was nothing at all for her, when so requested, to cause the living or the dead to appear in a mirror or upon the fingernail of a newborn child.

"She had a reputation for transforming men into animals, and for six years was said to have made use of a sacristan in the form of an ass. This was really and truly supposed to have happened. I never could make out how she did it, but those who are in a position to know say that the stories they tell about old-time sorceresses who changed men into beasts are readily to be explained: it was simply that, with their beauty and caresses, they attracted the men in such a manner as to win their love and subject them to their will, after which they employed them for any purpose they saw fit just as if they had been beasts.

"But in you, my son, I perceive that the opposite has hap-

pened; for though you are a rational being, I now behold you in
the likeness of a dog—unless it is all a result of the science they
call magic, which causes one thing to take on the appearance of
another. But be that as it may, what grieves me is the fact that
neither I nor your mother, who were pupils of the worthy Camacha, ever came to know as much as she did. This was not due
to any lack of intelligence, ability, or courage on our part, for we
had enough of all that and to spare, but was rather owing to
Camacha's maliciousness, for she was never willing to teach us the
more important things but reserved them for herself.

"Your mother, my lad, was called Montiela, and next to Camacha she was the most famous of us all. My name is Cañizares,
and if I am not as wise as those two were, at least I was the equal
of either of them in the matter of laudable ambition. It is true that,
when it came to entering a circle and shutting yourself up in it
with a legion of devils, your mother could vie with Camacha
herself. I was always a little timid and was content with half a
legion. But—peace be to both of them—in the matter of manu-
facturing those ointments that we witches use I would not take
second place to either of them nor to all those who follow and
observe our rules.

"I would have you know, my son, that as I saw my life flitting
away on the light wings of time, I have wished to leave behind me
all those vicious practices of sorcery in which I was immersed
for so many years, retaining only the desire to be a simple witch,
a practice that is very hard to leave off. Your mother did the same.
She gave up many of her evil ways and performed many good
deeds in this life, yet in the end she died a witch, and not from
sickness of any sort but from grief over what her teacher Camacha had done to her; for Camacha, upon perceiving that her

pupil was coming to know as much as she, or for some other reason, was jealous of her.

"Your mother at the time was pregnant, and when the hour of delivery came it was Camacha who with her own hands received the progeny—a pair of puppy dogs! As soon as she laid eyes on them she said, 'There is something evil here, some villainy, but I am your friend, sister Montiela, and I will conceal what you have just brought forth. All you have to do is to think about getting well, and you may rest assured that this disgraceful occurrence will be buried in silence itself. Do not let it worry you in the least, for you know, and I know, that for a long time now you have had nothing to do with anyone unless it was your lover, Rodríguez the laborer, and so this canine birth must come from some other source and there is something mysterious about it.' [61]

"Your mother and I (for I was present all the while) were amazed at this weird occurrence. Camacha went away, taking the puppies with her, and I stayed to look after Montiela, who could not believe that this event had really occurred. Then at last Camacha died, and when her last hour came she sent for your mother and told her how out of spite she had transformed the sons into dogs, adding that Montiela should not worry about it since they would be restored to their natural state when they least expected it. This, however, could not be until with their own eyes they should have beheld the fulfillment of this prophecy:

> " 'They shall return to their true form
>   when the haughty who have been exalted
>   are suddenly cast down and the humble
>   are lifted up by an able hand.' [62]

"That was what Camacha, at the time of her death, told your mother, as I was saying. Your mother took it all down in writing and memorized it as well, and I did the same in order that I might be able to repeat it to one of you if I ever had the opportunity. With the object of coming to know you, whenever I caught sight of any dogs of your color I called them by your mother's name, not because I expected them to recognize that name but merely to see if they would answer when addressed in so unusual a fashion. This evening, when I saw you performing so many tricks and heard them refer to you as 'the Wise Dog,' and again when you raised your head to look at me as I called to you out there in the garden, I came to believe that you were Montiela's son, and it is with the greatest pleasure that I tell you these things together with what you must do to recover your original form. I only wish it were as easy as Apuleius makes it out to be in his *Golden Ass*; for, according to him, all you have to do is eat a rose.

"Your recovery depends not upon your own diligence but upon the actions of other persons. What you should do, my son, is to commend yourself to God in your heart and wait for this prophecy, or better, this riddle, to be swiftly and happily fulfilled. Inasmuch as it was the worthy Camacha who uttered it, there can be no doubt that it will be, and you and your brother, if he is still alive, will find yourselves restored to that form which you desire. I am sorry that I am so near my end that I shall not be able to see it. Many times I have wanted to ask my billy goat how it would come out for you, but I did not venture to do so, for he never gives me a straight answer but replies in twisted sentences that may mean many things.

"The same is true of our lord and master. There is no use asking him anything, since with one truth he mingles a thousand lies. Judging from what I have been able to gather from his responses, he knows nothing for a certainty of what is to come but can only guess at it; yet it spite of it all he keeps us witches so under his spell that, though he plays innumerable pranks upon us, we are unable to leave him. We go to meet him in a large field that is a long way from here. There we find a huge throng of people, made up of witches and wizards, and there it is that we gorge ourselves with food, and other things happen which, in all truth—I swear to God and upon my soul—I should not dare to tell you as they are so filthy and loathesome that they would be an offense to your chaste ears.

"There is a prevalent belief that we attend these meetings only in our imaginations and that the devil merely pictures for us all those things that we afterward relate as having happened to us. Others take the contrary view and maintain that we really do go, in body and in soul. As for myself, I hold that both opinions are true, and that we do not know when we go in one way or the other, for the reason that everything that takes place in our imaginations happens so intensely that it is impossible for us to distinguish between the imaginary and the real. Those gentlemen the inquisitors who have arrested and questioned some of us can tell you about that, and I believe they will bear me out in what I have just said.[63]

"But I, my son, have done all I could to get away from my sins, and with this purpose in view I became a matron. I look after the poor, and some of them when they die leave me a bit to live on, or else I find it among their rags, for I am in the habit of going through their clothes very carefully. I pray but little and only in public; in private, I still indulge in backbiting. It is better for me to be a hypocrite than an open sinner, so that my apparent good deeds of the present may blot out the memory of the evil ones I committed in the past. In short, a feigned holiness does no harm to anyone else but only to the one who employs it.[64]

"Look you, my son Montiel, this is the advice I give you: always be as good as you can, but if you have to be bad, do your best not to appear so. I am a witch—there is no denying that; and the same is true of your mother, who was both a witch and a sorceress; yet the good appearance that we both kept up preserved our reputation in the sight of the world. Three days before she died the two of us attended a great devils' outing in a valley of the Pyrenees, yet despite all this, as she lay on her deathbed, she was so calm and tranquil that, if it had not been for a few grimaces that she made a quarter of an hour before she rendered up her soul, you might have thought that she was lying upon a bed of flowers.

"Her two sons were a burden on her heart, and even at the point of death she refused to forgive Camacha, so firm and resolute was she in such matters as that. I was the one who closed her lids and went with her to the grave. I left her there and have never seen her since, but I have not lost the hope of laying eyes upon her once again before I die; for it is said here in the village that certain ones have seen her wandering about the cemeteries and the crossroads in various disguises, and it may be that I shall meet her. In that case, I shall ask her what she would have me do to lighten the load upon her conscience."

Everything the old woman said in praise of the one she asserted was my mother was a stab through the heart for me. I felt like falling upon her and tearing her to pieces with my teeth, and if I refrained from doing so it was because I did not like to see her taken by death in such a state of sin. She ended by remarking that she planned to anoint herself that night and go to one of her usual meetings. While there, she meant to ask her master what was to happen to me. I was on the point of inquiring what the ointments were of which she was speaking, and she at once answered me just as if she had read my mind.

"This ointment that we witches use," she informed me, "is composed of the juice of very cold herbs and not, as is commonly believed, of the blood of infants that we have strangled. In this connection you may ask me what pleasure or profit the devil derives from having us slay those tender young creatures, since he knows that, being innocent and without sin, having already been baptized, they will go straight to Heaven, and he is especially pained over every Christian soul that escapes him. To this the only answer I can give you is the old proverb: 'There are those who, in order to gouge out their enemy's eye, would give both their own.'

"He does it on account of the grief that he inflicts on the parents by killing their young, for no greater sorrow is to be conceived. The thing that matters most to him is to accustom us to committing so cruel and perverse a sin; and all this God permits as a punishment for our transgressions, since I know by experience that without His permission the devil is unable to harm an ant. By way of showing you the truth of this, I once asked the devil to destroy one of my enemy's vineyards, and he replied that he could not touch so much as a leaf inasmuch as God did not will it.

"From what I have said, it should be clear to you, when you are a man, that all the misfortunes that come to us, to kingdoms, cities, and peoples, such as sudden death, shipwreck, calamities of every sort of the kind that are commonly known as acts of God —all these come from the hand of the Almighty and are willed by Him; whereas other evils and disasters where blame is to be imputed come from and are caused by ourselves. God is sinless; from which it is to be inferred that it is we who are the authors of sin in thought, word, and deed, with God, as I have said, permitting it all by reason of our waywardness of heart.

"By now, my son, in case you understand me, you must be wondering who taught me my theology, and you doubtless are saying to yourself, 'Devil take the old whore! Seeing that she knows so much, and knows that God is more ready to forgive sins than to permit them, why does she not leave off being a witch and return to Him?' To this I will answer, just as if you had asked me, that vice becomes second nature and witchcraft is something that enters into our blood and bones. It is marked by a great ardor, and at the same time it lays such a chill upon the soul as to benumb its faith and cause it to forget its own well-being, so that it no longer remembers the terrors with which God threatens it nor the glories of Heaven that He holds out to it.

"In short, seeing that it is a sin that is concerned with carnal pleasure, it must of necessity deaden, stupefy, and absorb the senses, so that they are unable to perform their wonted functions, and thus the soul, being left helpless, weak, and dejected, is no longer capable of entertaining any worthy thought but remains sunken in the profound abyss of its own misery with no desire to accept the hand that God out of His mercy extends to it in order to help it to rise. I have one of those souls of the kind I have described to you. I see and understand everything, but carnal pleasure keeps my will enchained, and I always have been and always shall be evil.

"But no more of this. Let us come back to the question of ointments. As I was saying, they are so cold as to deprive us of all sensation when we rub ourselves with them, and as a result we remain stretched out naked upon the floor; and then it is, they say, that we imagine as happening all those things that seem to us to be really occurring. Other times, after we have put on the ointment, we are transformed (in our own minds at least) and are changed into roosters, owls, or ravens, and in such shapes we go to the spot where our master is waiting for us and there resume our original forms and enjoy such pleasures as I refrain from mentioning, for the reason that the memory is scandalized at recalling them and the tongue avoids relating them. With it all, I am a witch and with the cloak of hypocrisy cover all my many faults. The truth is that if some esteem and honor me as a good woman, there are many who by way of recrimination whisper in my ear that reproachful name [65] which in times past was bestowed on your mother and me by an angry judge—he vented his wrath through an executioner who, not having been bribed, exerted the full power and severity of his office upon our backs.

"But all that is a thing of yesterday; for everything has an end, memories are no more, a life cannot be lived over again, tongues grow tired, and fresh happenings cause us to forget those that have gone before. I am a matron now and am careful to keep up appearances, my ointments afford me a little pleasure now and then, and I am not so old but that I may live for yet another year, even though I am seventy-five. On account of my age, however, I can no longer fast, I cannot pray, as it gives me a dizziness in the head, and my legs are so weak that I do not go on pilgrimages. I do not give alms either, for I am poor; nor am I capable of any worthy deed, for one must first have good thoughts, and I am too fond of backbiting and slander. And so it is my affections are evil; but for all of that, I know that God is good and merciful and that He knows what is to become of me. But let us leave off such talk as this, for it really makes me very sad. Come with me, my son, and you shall see me put on my ointment; for 'sorrows with bread are sweet,' and 'be sure to be at home when good luck comes your way,' since 'while you are laughing you are not crying,' [66] by all of which I mean to say that even though the pleasures with which the devil provides us are false and seeming ones, nevertheless they appear to us as pleasures, and carnal delight is greater when imagined than it is when enjoyed, whereas in the case of real pleasures just the opposite must be the case."

As she ended this long harangue she took up the lamp and entered another room, which was smaller than the first one. I followed her, torn with conflicting emotions, astonished at what I had just heard and expected to see. Cañizares hung the lamp up on the wall and then in great haste undressed down to her chemise. She snatched up a glazed pot that stood in one corner, and put her hand into it, muttering something between her teeth, and anointed herself from her feet all the way up to her head (she wore no headdress). Before she finished, she told me that, whether her body remained senseless in that room or disappeared from it, I was not to be frightened but was to wait there until the next morning in order to hear news of what was yet to happen to me before I became a man. I nodded my head in assent, and with that she stopped anointing herself and stretched out on the floor like a dead woman. I brought my mouth close to hers but could not make out any sign of breathing.

One thing I must confess to you, friend Cipión: I was very much frightened at finding myself shut up in such close quarters

with that creature lying there before me. I will try to describe
her for you as best I can. More than seven feet tall, she was a
skeleton covered by a dark, hairy, shriveled skin. Her belly was
of parchment and hung halfway down her thighs, thus covering
her shameful parts. Her breasts were two ox bladders, dry and
wrinkled, her lips were blackened, her teeth clenched, her nose
hooked and bony, her eyes protruding, her hair disheveled, her
cheeks hollow, her throat skinny, and her bosom sunken. In short,
she was a diabolical wraith.

I stared at her long and hard, and fear soon took possession of
me as I beheld that evil vision and thought of the still worse occupation upon which her soul was engaged. I felt like biting her to
see if I could bring her out of her trance but could find no part
of her that did not nauseate me too much. In spite of this, I seized
her by one of her heels and dragged her out into the courtyard,
but she still gave no sign of consciousness. As I looked up at the
sky and found myself in an open place, my fear left me, or at least
was diminished to such an extent that I had the courage to wait
and see what the outcome of this evil old woman's expedition
would be and what she would have to tell me concerning my own
affairs.

Meanwhile I kept asking myself: how is it that this old hag is
at once so wicked and so wise? How is it that she is able to distinguish between acts of God and those catastrophes for which
men are to blame? How does she come to know so much about
God and speak of Him so often while her works are those of the
devil? Why does she sin so much out of pure malice, not being
able to offer the excuse of ignorance?

With thoughts such as these the night passed and the day came,
to find us there in the middle of the patio. She was still uncon-

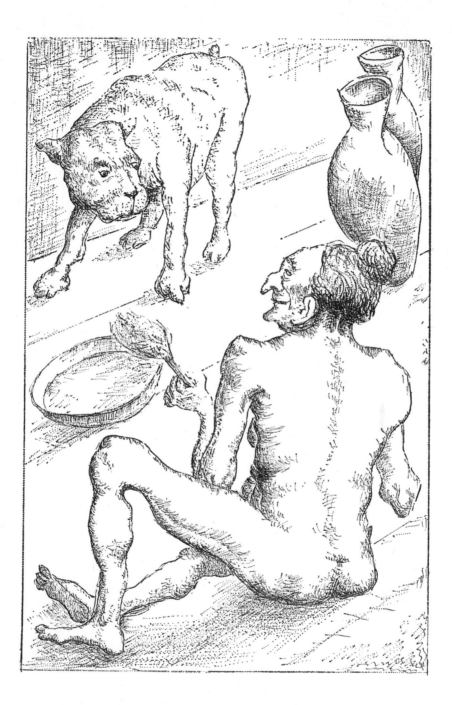

scious, and I was still squatting on my haunches close beside her, gazing attentively at her fearfully ugly features. The people from the hospital now came running out, and, seeing this picture, some of them exclaimed, "The pious Cañizares is dead! Just see how thin and disfigured she is as a result of the penance she has done!" Others had sufficient presence of mind to feel her pulse, and upon finding that she was not dead concluded that she must be in some holy trance or state of ecstasy. Still others said, "That old whore undoubtedly must be a witch; she must have anointed herself, for the saints in their ecstasies are never so immodest, and in any event, those of us who know her best look upon her as being a sorceress rather than a saint."

Certain curious ones came up to stick pins into her flesh from head to foot, but this did not succeed in awakening the sleeper, nor did she come to herself until along about seven o'clock. Perceiving that she had been stuck full of holes like a sieve and that her heels had been bitten and her body bruised by being dragged out from her room, and seeing all those eyes fixed upon her, she became aware of the truth, realizing that I was the one who was responsible for her disgrace. She accordingly threw herself upon me and, seizing my throat in both her hands, endeavored to strangle me as she screamed, "O ungrateful, ignorant, and malicious villain! And is this the pay I get for all the favors I did your mother and meant to do for you?" Being in danger of losing my life from the claws of that fierce harpy, I shook her off me and, seizing her by the long folds of her belly, I worried and dragged her all over the yard while she screamed for the bystanders to free her from the teeth of this evil spirit.

The old woman's words led most of them to believe that I must be one of those demons who are constantly envious of good

Christians. Some of them ran up to sprinkle me with holy water, some would have liked to pull me off her but did not dare, others cried out by way of conjuring me, the old woman kept on screaming, I sunk my teeth in deeper, the uproar increased, and my master, who had come up to see what the trouble was about, was in despair at hearing them say that I was a devil. Others still, who knew nothing of exorcisms, came running with three or four clubs and with them began making the sign of the cross over my loins. Tired of the joke by this time, I let go the old woman and in three jumps was in the street and in a few more was out of town, followed by a host of small boys shouting, "Get out of the way! Get out of the way! The Wise Dog has gone mad!" Others cried, "He's not mad! He's a demon in the form of a dog."

Following this beating, I left the town at top speed, pursued by many who must have been convinced that I was a demon as much by reason of the things they had seen me do as on account of the words the old woman had spoken when she awoke from her unholy slumbers. I was in such a hurry to flee and get out of her sight that they believed there was something demonic about the way in which I disappeared. In six hours' time I had covered a dozen leagues, and then I came to a gypsy camp which was in a field near Granada. There I rested a while; for some of the gypsies recognized me as the Wise Dog and were glad enough to take me in. They hid me in a cave, in case anyone should come looking for me, it being their intention as I afterward learned to make money with me just as my master the drummer had done. I stayed with them for twenty days, and in the course of that time had a chance to study their customs and mode of life, which, since they are quite out of the ordinary, I feel I ought to describe for you.

CIPIÓN: Before you go any further, Berganza, it would be well for us to pause and consider what the witch told you and see if it is the truth to which you are giving credence or if it is not rather a big hoax. Look here: it is utterly nonsensical to believe that Camacha could change men into beasts and that the sacristan, in the shape of an ass, served her all those years as they say he did. These things and others like them are nothing but humbuggery, lies, or illusions on the part of the devil; and if it seems to us at this moment that we have some little understanding and power of reason, whereas in reality we are but dogs or at least appear to be such, we have already agreed that this is a portentous and unheard-of case, and though it seems to us tangible enough, we should not really believe it until the event has shown us where the truth lies.

Do you wish to see things as they are more clearly? Then consider the foolish circumstances upon which, according to Camacha, our recovery depends. Those sayings of hers that you take to be prophecies are nothing more than old wives' tales—like that of the headless horse or the wand of virtues—of the kind that are told at the fireside on long winter nights.[67] Had they been anything else, they would have been fulfilled long ago, unless it is that her words are to be taken in what I have heard called an allegorical sense, that is to say, unless they have a meaning that differs from the literal one while at the same time resembling it. Let us look at those verses:

> "They shall return to their true form
> when the haughty who have been exalted
> are suddenly cast down and the humble
> are lifted up by an able hand."

Taking them in the sense that I have mentioned, the meaning to me appears to be that we shall recover our rightful form when we observe that those who yesterday were at the height of Fortune's wheel are today cast down and trampled under foot, being regarded as of little account by those who once esteemed them, while others, who not two hours ago had no other function than that of serving to increase the population of the earth, are now so exalted that we lose sight of them entirely, and where once they were little and shrunken they are now so far above us that they are out of reach.

If our restoration to our original form depends on this, then it is something that we have already witnessed and are witnessing all the time. But I believe that Camacha's verses are to be taken not in an allegorical but in a literal sense, and that the remedy for our plight does not depend on them at all, since we have often seen them fulfilled and, as you will note, we are as much dogs as we always were. This means that Camacha was playing a hoax, that Cañizares was a trickster, and that Montiela was at once foolish, cunning, and malicious—if I may be pardoned for speaking that way of our mother, or rather of your mother, for I will not have her for mine. In my opinion, what is meant by those verses is a game of ninepins, in which those pins that are standing are quickly cast down and those that have fallen are raised by the hand of one who is able to do it. Stop and think, then, as to whether or not in the course of our lives we have ever seen a game of ninepins, and if, having seen one, we have thereupon become men again, assuming that it what we really are.

BERGANZA: I admit that you are right, brother Cipión, and that you are wiser than I thought. From what you say I am led to believe that everything we have gone through and are going through now is a dream, and that we are but dogs, after all; but let us not for that reason fail to enjoy the blessing of speech that is ours and the invaluable faculty of being able to converse like human beings as long as we can. Therefore, I take it, it will not bore you to hear me relate what happened to me with the gypsies who hid me in a cave.

CIPIÓN: I shall be glad to listen to you, with the understanding that you are to listen to me when I tell you the story of my own life, if such be the will of Heaven.

BERGANZA: What I did during the time I was with the gypsies was to observe their numerous tricks, frauds, and impostures, and the thefts which all of them, male and female alike, committed from the time they were out of swaddling clothes and able to walk. You realize, do you not, how many of them there are, scattered throughout Spain? They all know and are in communication with one another and pass the articles they have stolen back and forth among themselves. They yield obedience, greater than that which the King can command, to one whom they call a count. This count and all his successors bear the name of Maldonado. This is not for the reason that they come of that noble line, but is due to the fact that a page in the service of a certain gentleman of that name fell in love with a gypsy maid who would not grant her love in return unless he first became a gypsy and took her for his wife. The page did so, and the gypsies liked him so well that they made him their overlord whom they were to obey, and as a token of this vassalage they share with him the proceeds from all the thefts of any importance that they commit.

By way of filling their idle lives, they engage in iron work and fashion implements that will aid them in their thieving; and so it is you will see the men going through the streets hawking tongs, gimlets, and hammers, while the women sell tripods and shovels. All the women are midwives, and in this respect, they have an advantage over ours since they are able to give birth without attendants or expense. They wash the newborn infants in cold water, and all gypsies, from the day they are born to the day they die, are taught to endure the harshest inclemencies of the weather. As a result, they are all sturdy jumpers, runners, and dancers. They always marry among themselves so that their evil ways may not become known to outsiders. The women are respectful toward their husbands, and there are very few who ever trifle with those who are not of their own race. When they beg alms, they make use of tricks and buffoonery instead of appealing to charity, and inasmuch as no one trusts them, they keep faith with none and pride themselves on their idle, vagabond life.

Almost never—if ever—do I recall having seen a gypsy woman taking communion at the foot of the altar, although I have many times been in churches. All that they think of is how to deceive and where they are going to commit their next theft. They boast of their thieving exploits and the manner in which they performed them. Thus, I one day heard a gypsy telling the others of the trick he had played upon a peasant. This gypsy had a bobtailed ass on which he had grafted a false tail that looked like the beast's very own. He took it to market, where a peasant bought it for ten ducats; and having sold it and pocketed the money, he re-marked that he had another ass at home, a brother to this one, that he would sell at an even better bargain. The peasant told him to go and fetch it, saying he would be glad to buy it, adding that in the meanwhile he would take the one he had just purchased to his lodgings.

The peasant went away, and the gypsy followed him and some

way or other contrived to steal the ass he had sold. He at once took off the false tail, leaving the beast with its stump, and at the same time he changed the packsaddle and the halter; then he went to look for the peasant before the latter should have found that the ass he had taken back with him was missing. Within a few moments the fellow had made a second purchase and went to his lodgings to close the deal, where he discovered that the "first" ass was missing. Although he was none too bright, he suspected that the gypsy had stolen it and he accordingly refused to pay a second time.

The gypsy, however, produced as witnesses those who had received the tax on the first transaction, and they swore that he had sold the peasant an ass with a very long tail, quite different from the second one. A constable was present all the while, and he supported the gypsy so strongly that there was nothing for the victim to do but pay for the ass twice over.

They had tales to tell of other thefts they had committed, almost all of them involving beasts of burden, this being a form of knavery in which they are past masters, having had a great deal of practice at it. The short of it is, they are a thoroughly bad lot, and although many very wise judges have dealt harshly with them, they have not on that account mended their ways.

At the end of twenty days they set out to take me to Murcia, going by way of Granada, where the drummer who had been my master and his company were stationed. As soon as they learned of this, the gypsies shut me up in a room of the inn where they were staying, but I overheard them talking about it, and inasmuch as I did not care for the journey on which they were taking me, I made up my mind to free myself. This I did; and, leaving Granada, I sought refuge in the garden of a Morisco, who was very glad to have me; and I was even more glad, thinking that all he wanted me for was to watch his garden, an occupation that was much less work than guarding a flock. Since in our case there was no necessity of arguing over wages, it was easy for the Morisco to find a servant and me a master.

I stayed with him for more than a month, not because I was fond of that kind of a life but rather because I found pleasure in observing the life my master led, which was similar to that of all the Moriscos in Spain. Oh, what things I could tell you, friend Cipión, of that Moorish riffraff, if I were not afraid that it would take me a couple of weeks to do so! And if I were to go into details, I should not be through in a couple of months. But I will tell you something in a general way of what I saw and made special note of while dwelling among these good people.

It is only by a miracle if you find among all of them one who really believes in the holy law of Christianity. Their only concern is to hoard and accumulate money, and in order to do so they work hard and eat practically nothing. If a real comes into their possession, they immediately condemn it to perpetual imprisonment and eternal darkness, with the result that, always making money and never spending any, they pile up the largest amount of it that is to be found anywhere in Spain. They are Spain's strongbox, its moths, its magpies, its weasels: everything that they get hold of they devour or hide away. Remember how many of them there are, and that each day they get something and lay something by, whether little or much; remember also that a slow fever can put an end to life as surely as a raging one; and, finally, bear in mind that the number of these hoarders is constantly increasing and will keep on doing so to an indefinite extent, as experience has shown.

There is no such thing as chastity among them. Neither the men nor the women ever enter convents or monasteries, but they all marry and multiply, and their sober mode of life increases their generative powers. Their numbers are not diminished either by war or overwork. They rob us on the sly, and by selling the fruit of our inheritance they grow rich. They have no servants, but all wait upon themselves. They do not spend money upon educating their sons, for their only science is that of robbing us. From the twelve sons of Jacob who entered Egypt, so I have heard it said, there had sprung six hundred thousand males, not counting the women and children, by the time Moses led them out of bondage. From this it may be inferred how rapidly the Moriscos multiply, whose numbers are infinitely greater to begin with.

CIPIÓN: A remedy has been sought for all those evils that you have pointed out or vaguely hinted at—and I am well aware that there are many more even greater ones of which you have said nothing—but up to now they have not hit upon the proper measures to be taken, although our state has most wise and zealous protectors who, aware that Spain is nourishing in its bosom such vipers as these, with God's help are bound to find a prompt and speedy redress for so great a wrong. Go on with what you have to say.

BERGANZA: My master being a miser, as all those of his kind are, he gave me only millet bread to eat and a little thin soup, which was his own ordinary fare; but this penury on his part was to bring me a very strange and pleasurable experience, as you shall hear. Each morning at dawn a young man came out to seat himself at the foot of one of the many pomegranate trees in the garden. He was clad in a robe of black baize, shiny and thread-bare, and appeared to be a student. He busied himself writing in a notebook and from time to time would strike his forehead with the palm of his hand, bite his fingernails, and gaze up at the sky, while at other times he was so lost in revery that he did not stir hand or foot or so much as bat an eyelid, so great was the rapture in which he appeared to be absorbed.

I crept up to him once without his seeing me and heard him muttering to himself, and after a while he cried out in a loud voice, "Praise the Lord, that is the best octave I ever composed!" With this he started scribbling furiously in his notebook and seemed so happy that I at once realized the poor fellow was a poet. I then went through my usual affectionate tricks to assure him of my gentleness and cast myself down at his feet, while he, feeling that I meant him no harm, went on with his thoughts and once more began scratching his head, going off into a trance, and writing down what came into his mind.

At this point another youth, very spruce and well dressed, entered the garden. In his hand he had some papers which he read from time to time. "Have you finished the first act?" he inquired, coming up to the other young man.

"I have just this moment given it the finest ending that could be imagined," was the poet's reply.

"And how have you ended it?" the other one wanted to know.

"In this way: His Holiness the Pope comes out, in full pontificals, accompanied by a dozen cardinals all clad in purple robes; for at the time the action takes place it is the season for *mutatio caparum*,[68] when the cardinals do not wear red but purple; and so, in order to be true to life, it is absolutely necessary that these be properly attired. This is a very important point where the writing of plays is concerned, and by not observing it there are many who make a lot of nonsensical blunders. As for me, I could not go wrong, having read the entire Roman Ceremonial to make sure I was correct in the matter of vestments."

"But where," asked the other, "do you think my manager is going to find purple robes for a dozen cardinals?"

"If he deprives me of a single one of them," declared the poet, "I'd as soon think of giving him my play as I would of flying. Good Lord, and are we going to lose the chance for such a magnificent spectacle as that? Just imagine what a sight it will be to behold the Supreme Pontiff himself on the stage with a dozen grave cardinals and the other attendants that he will necessarily have in his train! Heavens! Why, it will be one of the greatest and most sublime exhibitions that was ever seen in connection with any play, not excluding *Daraja's Nosegay*." [69]

From this I understood that one of them was a poet, the other an actor. The latter was advising the author to reduce somewhat the number of cardinals if he did not wish to make it impossible for the manager to produce his play. To this the poet replied that they ought to be thankful that he had not introduced the entire conclave of prelates upon this memorable occasion which he meant to immortalize for posterity. The player laughed and went about his own business, which was that of studying a role in a new comedy. As for the poet, after he had jotted down a few couplets of his magnificent production he slowly and carefully took from his pocket some bread crumbs and about twenty raisins, as nearly as I could count them, although I am inclined to doubt that there were so many after all, for the bread that was mixed with them made them appear to be more than they were. Blowing off the crumbs, he ate the raisins, stems and all; [70] for I did not see him throw anything away. To these he added bits of bread which, having turned a purple hue from the lining of his pocket, had a moldy look and were so hard that he could not soften them up enough to swallow them though he chewed them over and over again. All of which was to my advantage; for he now tossed them to me, saying, "Here, take them, and much good may they do you."

"Behold," I said to myself, "the nectar and ambrosia that this poet gives me, on which, so the poets tell us, Apollo and the other gods are nourished up there in the heavens." The truth of the matter is, though poets for the most part are wretchedly poor, I was needier still, being obliged to eat what he tossed me. So long as he continued working on his play, he did not fail to come to the garden and I did not lack crumbs; for he shared them with me most generously, and afterward we would go to the well, where I would lap up the water while he made use of a pitcher, and together we satisfied our thirst like a couple of kings.

But at last the poet stopped coming, and my hunger became so great that I resolved to leave the Morisco and go to the city to see if I could change my luck. As I entered the town I caught sight of my poet friend coming out of the famous monastery of San Jerónimo. The moment he saw me, he came up to me with open arms, while I displayed fresh signs of joy at having found him once more. He at once began emptying his pockets of crusts of bread, softer than those he used to bring to the garden, and he gave them to me without first having chewed them himself, which enabled me to satisfy my hunger. These tender crusts and the fact that I had seen him coming out of a monastery led me to suspect that his muse, like that of so many others of his kind, was a shamefaced beggar.

He took the road into the town, and I followed him, with the intention of adopting him as my master if he was willing, for I thought that these leftovers of his would maintain me in royal fashion, seeing that there is no greater or better purse than that of Charity, whose generous hands are never poor. In this respect I cannot agree with the proverb which says "The hardhearted give more than the destitute"; just as if the hardhearted miser would give you anything, whereas the one who is destitute but generous at least gives you his best wishes if he has nothing more to offer.

After a while we stopped at the house of a theatrical manager who, as I recall, was named Angulo the Bad, not to be confused with that other Angulo, who was not a manager but one of the best actors that the stage has ever known, then or now.[71] The whole company was assembled to listen to a reading of the play my master (for by this time I regarded him as such) had written; but in the middle of the first act they began leaving, one or two at a time, until the manager and I were the only audience that was left. I am an ass where matters of poetry are concerned, but it seemed to me that this piece must have been composed by Satan himself for the total ruin and perdition of the author, who, seeing himself deserted in this fashion, was swallowing hard and, it may be (I should not wonder if such was the case), was anticipating the disgrace about to befall him; for all the players, more than twelve in number, now returned and without saying a word laid hold of my poet friend, and if it had not been for the manager's cries and entreaties together with the authority that he wielded, they undoubtedly would have tossed the poor fellow in a blanket then and there.

I was astounded, the manager disconcerted, the players merry, and the poet glum. With a somewhat wry face the author picked up his comedy, stuffed it in his bosom, and stalked out with much composure, muttering, "It is not well to cast pearls before swine." I was ashamed and had no desire to follow him even if I had been able to do so, for the manager bestowed so many caresses on me that I was obliged to remain with him, and in less than a month I was cutting a great figure as an actor in interludes and pantomimes. They put a muzzle on me and taught me to fall upon any of the characters on the stage whom they wished me to attack. Most interludes, you know, end with clubbings, but in my master's company they ended with his sicking me on the actors, and I would knock them all down and tumble them about, to the great delight of the ignorant and my master's profit.

O Cipión, how could anyone tell you what I saw in that company of actors and other companies of which I formed a part! Since it is not possible to make a short story of it, I shall have to leave it for another day, assuming there is to be another day in which we shall be able to communicate with each other. You see, do you not, how long a time it has taken me already, all the many and varied things that have happened to me, all the roads I have traveled, the many masters I have had? Well, all that you have heard is as nothing compared with what I could tell you of the things I observed and noted among these people: their life and conduct, their manners and occupations, their work, their idleness, their ignorance, and their cleverness, along with a multitude of other circumstances, some of which would be for your ear alone, while others ought to be proclaimed in public by way of disillusioning the many who idolize these fictitious characters with all their false finery and artifices.

CIPIÓN: I can see you have a large field there, Berganza, and I am of the opinion it would be better to make a separate story of it and tell it at your leisure, not hurriedly.

BERGANZA: Very well, but listen. It was with one of those companies I have mentioned that I came to this city of Valladolid, where, during the performance of an interlude, I received a wound that nearly put an end to my life. Being muzzled, I was unable to avenge myself at the time, and afterward I did not feel like doing so, since a revenge that is thought out shows cruelty and malice aforethought. The profession of an actor irked me, not on account of the work involved but because of the abuses connected with it that call for correction and punishment. However, I was in a position to perceive these rather than to remedy them, and so I made up my mind to put them out of my sight and take refuge in some religious house, as those persons do who would leave their vices behind them when they can no longer practice them—better late than never.

I may tell you then that, observing you one night carrying the lantern with that good Christian Mahudes, I saw how content you were and how just and righteous was your occupation, and, filled with envy of the right sort, I decided to follow in your footsteps. With that praiseworthy intention I placed myself in Mahudes's way, and he at once chose me for your companion and brought me to this hospital. As for the things that have happened to me since I came here, they are not so few but that it would require considerable time to tell them. I should especially like to tell you of a conversation I overheard on the part of four patients whom bad luck and want had brought to this place and who occupied neighboring beds. Please bear with me, for the story is a short one and very much to the point. And so, with your permission—

CIPIÓN: I grant it; but hurry up and finish, for it will soon be day, I think.

BERGANZA: I must explain that in one of those four beds, at the far end of this infirmary, there lay an alchemist, in the second a poet, in the third a mathematician, and in the fourth one of those persons who are known as planners.

CIPIÓN: Yes, I remember meeting some of that tribe.

BERGANZA: It was during the siesta hour last summer. The windows were closed, and I was taking the air beneath the bed of one of these patients when the poet began lamenting loudly his misfortunes. Asked by the mathematician what his complaint was, he replied as follows:

"Have I not good reason to complain? I have always observed the precept that Horace gives us in his *Art of Poetry*, namely, not to publish a work until ten years after it has been composed.[72] Well, I have a work on which I labored for twenty years, and it has been twelve years since I completed it. Its subject is an exalted one, the plot is excellent and highly original, the versification is stately, the episodes are entertaining, and the arrangement is marvelous, for the beginning, the middle, and the end are in perfect accord, the whole constituting a poem that is lofty, sonorous, heroic, delightful, and full of substance; yet with all of this, how is it that I have not found some prince to whom I can dedicate it—a prince, I mean to say, who is intelligent, generous, and magnanimous? Oh, how wretched and depraved is this age of ours!"

"What is the subject of your book?" inquired the alchemist.

"It deals," replied the poet, "with what Archbishop Turpin failed to tell us of King Arthur of England, together with a continuation of the Quest of the Holy Grail.[73] It is all written in heroic verse, partly in octaves and partly in blank verse, but all of it dactylically, that is to say, in dactyls consisting of nouns only, no verbs being permitted."

"I do not know much about poetry," said the alchemist, "and so I am unable to estimate the extent of your Grace's misfortune; but even though it were greater than it is, it could not equal mine. My trouble lies in not being able to find a prince who will support me and provide me with those instruments that the science of alchemy demands. Otherwise, I should now be rolling in gold and richer than any Midas, Crassus, or Croesus ever was."

The mathematician then spoke up. "Sir Alchemist," he said, "has your Grace tried the experiment of extracting silver from other metals?"

"I have not done so up to now," the alchemist answered him, "but I know that it is possible to do so, and it would take me less than two months to hit upon the philosophical stone by means of which silver and gold can be made from the same rock."

"You gentlemen," said the mathematician, have been making too much of your troubles! One of you has a book and is looking for a patron, and the other is near finding the philosophical stone; but what am I to say of my misfortune, which is so unique that there is none to compare with it? For twenty-two years now I have been in search of the fixed point.[74] Here I lose sight of it and there I find it again, and just when it seems to me that I have found it and it cannot possibly escape me, I suddenly discover I am so far from it that I truly am astonished. The same thing happens to me with the squaring of the circle.[75] I have come so near it that I cannot imagine why it is I do not have it in my pocket right now. And thus my pain is like that of Tantalus, who is near the fruit and yet dying of hunger, near the water, yet perishing of thirst. At certain moments I think that I have attained the truth, and again it is beyond my reach, and I once more have to start climbing that slope I have just descended with the stone of my labors on my back like another Sisyphus."

At this point the planner broke the silence that he had maintained up to then. "Poverty," he observed, "has brought together in this hospital four grumblers that would do honor to the Grand Turk himself.[76] Personally, I have no use for trades and professions that do not provide a means of support for those who follow them. I, gentlemen, am a deviser of plans, and on various occasions I have furnished His Majesty with many different schemes all of which would be to his benefit and without harm to the realm. At this moment I have a petition already drawn up in which I beg him to indicate the person to whom I may communicate a new plan of mine which would result in the liquidation of all his debts; but, judging from what has happened to my previous petitions, I feel certain that this one also will end up in the dustbin.

"But in order that your Graces may not take me for a crackbrain, I should like to tell you what my scheme is, even though I am thereby making it public. It consists in asking the Cortes to command all His Majesty's vassals between the ages of fourteen and sixty to fast on bread and water once a month, on whatever day may be selected and designated for that purpose, with the provision that all the money that would have been spent on that day for fruit, meat and fish, wine, eggs and vegetables, is to be paid in to His Majesty, under oath and without defrauding him of a single penny. In that way, in twenty years' time, he will be free of all debts and obligations.

"For if you make a count, as I have done, you will find that there are in Spain more than three million persons within those age limits, exclusive of the sick, the very old, and the very young,[77] none of whom at the lowest estimate spends less than a real and a half a day. However, I would set the figure at not more than a real, nor would I make it any less even in the case of those who live on fenugreek. And what do your Graces think of that? Are three million reales nothing at all? [78] And all this would benefit rather than harm the fasters, for they would thus be able to please Heaven and serve their King at one and the same time; and some of them might even find it good for their health. That is my plan, plain and simple. The collection could be made by parishes, without any expense for commissaries, who are the bane of our commonwealth." [79]

They all had a laugh at the planner and his plan, and he himself had to smile at his own foolishness, while I was astonished at what I had heard and I reflected that most persons of this sort come to die in hospitals.

CIPIÓN: Right you are, Berganza. Have you anything else to say?

BERGANZA: A couple of things, no more, and with that I shall be done, for I think the day is close at hand. One night my master went to beg alms at the house of the mayor [80] of that city, a fine gentleman and a very fine Christian. Since we were alone with him, I thought it would be a good opportunity to inform him of what I had heard an old man say who was a patient in this hospital. It concerned the means of remedying the harm that, as everyone knows, is done by those homeless girls who from want of any other occupation fall into evil ways—so evil that in summertime all the hospitals are filled with their victims. They constitute an intolerable plague and one that calls for a swift and efficacious remedy.

Well, as I was saying, I wanted to tell him this, and, thinking that I had the power of speech, I raised my voice to do so, but in place of uttering coherent sentences I barked so loudly and insistently that the mayor became angry and called to his servants to give me a beating and put me out. One of his lackeys, who had come running up when the master raised his voice, thereupon snatched up the first thing at hand, which chanced to be a water-cooler made of copper, and with it he flayed my ribs so hard that I still bear the marks of the blows he dealt me.

CIPIÓN: And do you complain of that, Berganza?

BERGANZA: And why should I not complain, when, as I told you, I can feel it yet, and especially in view of the fact that my good intentions did not deserve any such punishment as that?

CIPIÓN: Look you, Berganza, no one has any business meddling in what does not concern him. You were entirely too officious. You should remember that the advice of the poor, no matter how good it may be, is never taken; nor should the one who is poor and humble be so presumptuous as to undertake to advise those of high station, who think they know it all. Wisdom in the poor man is always overcast, want and misery being the clouds that darken it; and if by any chance it does shine through, it is looked upon as foolishness and treated with contempt.

BERGANZA: You are right, and, having learned by painful experience, I shall follow your advice hereafter. On another night we entered the house of a lady of importance who held in her arms a small dog of the kind known as lapdogs—it was so small that she might have hidden it in her bosom. When it saw me, it leaped from its mistress's arms and began barking at me and attacking me with such fearlessness that it did not stop until it had bitten my leg. I turned to look at it with annoyance and disgust,

saying to myself, "You little runt, if I only had you out in the street I would either pay no attention to you or else I would tear you to pieces with my teeth!" For I could not help reflecting how cowards and those of little spirit become bold and insolent when they are thus protected, and go out of their way to offend their betters.

CIPIÓN: We have an example of that in certain puny little men who dare to be insolent when under the protection of their masters; but if by any chance death or some other turn of fortune strikes down the tree against which they lean, their lack of real valor is at once manifested, since the truth is that their only worth is that conferred upon them by their patrons, whereas virtue and intelligence are always one and the same, naked or clothed, alone or in the company of others—true, they may suffer in public esteem, but their real worth is not thereby diminished.

But let us put an end to this conversation, for the light coming in through those chinks shows us that day is here, and tonight, unless we shall have lost this great blessing of speech, it will be my turn to tell the story of my life.

BERGANZA: Very well, and be sure that you come to this same spot.

NOTES

Notes

PROLOGUE

1. The pen portrait of himself that Cervantes gives us probably provided the basis for the painting of him that has been attributed to the artist Juan de Jáuregui (1583–1641), a canvas supposed to have been executed in the year 1600 and which was later accepted as authentic by the Spanish Royal Academy. It is clear from the author's own words that no portrait existed in 1613, three years before his death.

2. Cesare Caporali of Perusa had published a poem entitled *Viaggio in Parnaso*, in 1582; but Benedetto Croce has pointed out that the two works are quite different, Cervantes' being six times as long as the other.

3. Cervantes was sixty-six years of age in 1613.

RINCONETE AND CORTADILLO

The probable date of composition, according to F. Rodríguez Marín, is 1601–1602; according to James Fitzmaurice-Kelly, 1603–1604. There is in existence a manuscript, based upon a first draft and differing somewhat from the printed text, that was copied out, before 1609, for Cardinal Niño de Guevara by the prebendary of the cathedral of Seville, Francisco Porras de la Cámara (indicating that the princes of the Church were not above such reading as this). I have followed the text of the first edition (1613), correlated with the Madrid edition of 1614, as given in Rudolph Schevill and Adolfo Bonilla y San Martín, *Obras Completas de Miguel Cervantes Saavedra*.

The topography of the story is exact. The Molinillo inn at which the two lads meet was situated on the road from Toledo to Cordova; it was two leagues from Tartanedo and four leagues from Almodóvar del Campo; and the Alcalde inn, as stated, was half a league distant. Alcudia was a valley in the province of Ciudad Real. Fuenfrida (today Fuenfría), where Rinconete was born, was a pass in the Guadarrama Mountains formerly used by the Spanish kings upon their journeyings; it was three leagues from Segovia on the road to Toledo. The "pious village" from which Cortadillo came, between Medina del Campo and Salamanca, was doubtless Mollorido, seat of a bishopric. (I have followed the first-edition reading, "*piadoso lugar*," and not the one given by subsequent editors, "*en el Pedroso, lugar . . .*").

The allusions to sites in and about Seville are similarly accurate: the Customhouse Gate (puerta de la Aduana); the Arenal Gate (puerta del Arenal) and the Old Clothes Market (Baratillo) nearby; the Meat Market (Carnicería), the Fish Market (Pescadería), the plaza de San Salvador, the little square known as the Costanilla, or Slope, and the plaza de la Feria, or the Fair; the King's Garden (Huerta del Rey), the Bank of the Indies (Casa de Contratación), the Treasury (Casa de la Moneda), the plaza de la Alfalfa, the Golden Tower (Torre del Oro), the Castle Postern (postigo del Alcázar); San Sebastián field and the chapel of San Telmo, the calle de Tintores—all these places have been definitely located.

An attempt has even been made to identify Monipodio's house, and a late nineteenth-century scholar, Adolfo de Castro, would place it in the present calle de Troya, formerly the calle de la Cruz, as he finds that the courtyard of this house (No. 4) corresponds with Cervantes' description of the thieves' patio. The shrine of Our Lady of the Waters (Nuestra Señora de las Aguas) was in the church of El Salvador; it is still venerated today, as it had been long before Cervantes wrote. The crucifix of St. Augustine, a fine specimen of fourteenth-century Romanesque sculpture, was then to be found in the church bearing his name, but today it is preserved in the church of San Roque.

1. The word "*rincón*" means "nook" or "corner."
2. Vilhan, or Bilhan, was the legendary inventor of the game of cards.
3. From "*cortar*"—"to cut."
4. Expression used in entering upon a new undertaking.
5. The customary conclusion of a "fortune" as told by a gypsy.
6. That is, thieves.
7. In the original there is an untranslatable play on sounds here.
8. The literal meaning of Monipodio is a gang, in the underworld sense.
9. Reference is to hanging, flogging, and the galleys.
10. Theologies.
11. In the Spanish ("*ministros y contrayentes*") there is a jocular allusion to the marriage ceremony, through a play on the double meaning of "*ministros*"—"ministers" and "agents."
12. Trademark of the fifteenth-century swordmaker, Julián del Rey, a Moorish convert patronized by the King.
13. "*Naufragio*" ("shipwreck") is here a solecism for "*sufragio*," or "suffrage," in the ecclesiastical sense of an intercessory prayer or petition. For "swag" Monipodio says "*estupendo*" ("stupendous") in place of "*estipendio*" ("stipend"). On this passage, see p. 62 following. Rodríguez Marín finds these word plays unworthy of Cervantes.
14. "*Tormenta*" means "storm" and also "misfortune" or "reverse."

15. The meaning of *"ganchuelo"* is "a little hook."

16. This passage, in sixteenth-century thieves' jargon, has been freely rendered in an effort to give the general sense. A number of the terms are still in doubt.

17. The pickpocket puts in two fingers to ascertain the size of the pocket and what is in it, then all five to remove the contents.

18. The "house" here is the brothel.

19. Don Alonso Pérez de Guzmán el Bueno was governor of the city of Tarifa when it was besieged, in 1293, by Prince Don Juan of Castile, who had revolted against his brother, Sancho IV. Don Alonso's infant son had fallen into the hands of the enemy, and when Don Alonso was called upon to surrender or see his child slain, he detached his dagger from his belt and threw it down from the wall as a sign of defiance. The babe was slaughtered in front of his eyes. Cervantes is in error in referring to this son as being Alonso's only one.

20. The *"medio manto"* or *"manto negro doblado"* was the legally required garb of prostitutes.

21. *"Mojar la canal maestra"*—literally, "wet the main canal." Compare our expression "down the main hatch."

22. The sense of the name is "the earner" or "the winner." Silbatillo is a diminutive of *"silbato"*—"a whistle."

23. Escalanta is from *"escalar"*—"to climb" or "to enter surreptitiously."

24. Two arrobas would be eight and a half gallons; an azumbre is a little more than half a gallon—quite a drink for an old lady!

25. The white wine of Guadalcanal (there was also a red wine) was one of the most famous of sixteenth-century vintages.

26. From *"pipa"*—"cask" or "hogshead," in allusion to her drinking capacity.

27. St. Lucy, virgin martyr who had her eyes burned out, is especially venerated by those afflicted with diseases of the eye.

28. The bread of Gandul, renowned in the sixteenth and seventeenth centuries, came from a little village of that name near Seville.

29. The Tagarete was a stream that formed a moat at Seville and there emptied into the Guadalquivir. Its waters are said to have been rather foul-smelling. According to Rodríguez Marín, the implication is that the Tagarete of the story was a *tributary* of Monipodio.

30. *"Respecto"*—euphemism for "pimp"; in argot, the *respecto* was a sword.

31. The sense is, a thief who sells what others have stolen.

32. Proverbial expression meaning to drink nine times.

33. She means a tiger of Hyrcania. The "Tarpeian mariner" is a pun on the first line of an old ballad: *"Mira, Nero, de Tarpeya,/A Roma como se ardía. . . ."* Ocaña is near Madrid.

34. The "tame doves" are servant maids.

35. An expression from the old markets, meaning to smash everything without regard to consequences.

36. Giving of the lie in this fashion was a common means of provocation among bullies; it has nothing to do with anything said by Chiquiznaque or Maniferro.

37. Where the weapons are carried.

38. Solecism for Judas Macabeo (Maccabaeus).

39. The use of the broom as a musical instrument is mentioned by a number of Spanish writers.

40. Negrofeo is Orfeo (Orpheus), Arauz is Euridice, Marión is Arion, while the other reference is to Amphion.

41. The *seguidilla* is a Spanish verse form consisting of a seven-line stanza with a complicated structure commonly based on assonance. The word has come to mean a popular air or dance tune. The lines in the original are in couplets. I have substituted a well-known English form.

42. That is, they worked for neither side, did not molest the "brotherhood."

43. "*De barrio.*"

44. "Love me, love my dog."

45. Executor.

46. "*Desmochado.*" His ear had probably been cut off as a punishment.

47. The vials, of course, contained offensive or injurious liquids; greasy, foul-smelling juniper oil is still occasionally employed for revenge by Andalusian peasants; the nailing up of the *sambenito*, or flame-colored robe, worn by penitents when going to the stake, amounted to an accusation of heresy or of being a Jew; the horns, indicating a cuckold, were employed at least as late as 1911 (Rodríguez Marín).

48. It was Cortadillo to whom this title was given.

49. "*Lobillo*," diminutive of "*lobo*"—"wolf" or, in jargon, "thief."

50. See note 13.

MAN OF GLASS

The date of composition has been given as 1604 or 1605. If the latter date is correct, it was probably written about the same time as "The Colloquy of the Dogs." I have followed Schevill and Bonilla's reproduction of the first-edition text (1613), disregarding the variants of the so-called Madrid edition of 1614. In the matter of notes and linguistic interpretation, I have drawn as usual on Rodríguez Marín and on the special edition of this tale by the modern editor Narciso Alonso Cortés.

1. As in all his fiction, Cervantes here is a realist in the matter of detail. Thus there is nothing improbable in Rodaja's being permitted to enroll at the University of Salamanca while acting as a servant to the two

wealthy students. As Alonso Cortés has pointed out, penniless youths of scholastic bent frequently maintained themselves in this fashion.

2. The word *"rodaja"* means "a small wheel."

3. The Spaniards, who wore dark clothes in town, donned showy garments for travel on the highway.

4. Macaronic Italian of the sort spoken by Spanish soldiers. "Landlord, prepare us a meal; come here, you rascal; bring on the *maccatella*, the chicken, and the macaroni." The meaning of *"maccatella"* (*"macarela"*) is uncertain; it was perhaps a dish composed of pounded meat balls. The correct Italian forms would be: *"Acconcia, patrone; passa quà, manigoldo; vengano la maccatella, li pollastri, e li maccheroni."*

5. Expression from the game of cards.

6. The soldiers dressed themselves, at their own expense, in gay-colored garments calculated to catch the eyes of the ladies.

7. *"Dios es Cristo":* the term implied swaggering bullies.

8. The famous poet Garcilaso de la Vega (1503?–1536) who was Cervantes' model.

9. Name given to the southeastern portion of the harbor of Genoa.

10. These wines are Italian vintages. Trebbiano was a sweet white wine from the banks of the Trebbia; Montefiascone came from the place of that name in papal territory; Asprino was a white wine of Capua or Naples; the wine of Candia (*malvasía*) was made of grapes grown on that island; Five Vineyards was from the place so named near Genoa; Vernaccia (or Guarnaccia) was from San Luchito; Centola was from the town of that name in the region of Naples; and Romanesco was from the Roman campagna.

11. Reference to Ciudad Real (literally, Royal City) and its wine.

12. These are well-known Spanish vintages. Those of Madrigal (Guadalajara), Alaejos, Esquivias, Alanís (near Seville), Membrilla, Ribadavia, and Descargamaría were white wines; those of Guadalcanal were white and red; that of Cazalla was a rather sweet red wine. The vintage of Coca is described by an early nineteenth-century writer as being "very bad and weak" (from the note in Schevill and Bonilla).

13. The famed Seven Hills of Rome were the Capitoline, the Palatine, the Aventine, the Esquiline, the Caelian, the Quirinal, and the Viminal. The Vatican was one of the five secondary mounts.

14. The "Seven Churches" were those of St. Peter, St. Paul, St. John Lateran, St. Sebastian, St. Mary (Santa Maria Maggiore), St. Lawrence, and Holy Cross.

15. That is, the room in which the Annunciation occurred. The allusion is to the Santa Casa, or House of the Virgin, in the cathedral of Loretto. It was said to have been transported by angels from Nazareth to Dalmatia in 1291, and from there to Loretto in 1295.

16. This is based upon the second report of Cortés, dated October 30, 1520, and printed in Seville in 1522.

17. Allusion to the proverb *"Del dicho a hecho hay mucho trecho"*— "It is a long way from saying to doing."

18. The word originally meant a student's notebook but came to mean a student or the servant to a student.

19. Among the Greeks and the Romans the quince was sacred to Venus and was a customary lover's gift.

20. The Monte Testaccio, near St. Paul's Gate, was a dumping place for broken crockery.

21. Proverbial expression, equivalent to saying, "Your troubles do not concern me."

22. Luke 23:28: "Daughters of Jerusalem, . . . weep for yourselves, and for your children." The implication is that her husband was not the father of her children.

23. Literal translation of *"Vidriera."*

24. "Domingo"—"Sunday"; "Sabado"—"Saturday." The implication is that the second man is a Jew.

25. The theme is a recurring one with Cervantes and has something of an autobiographical ring. See, for example, "The Jealous Old Man," in Sylvanus Griswold Morley's translation of the *Interludes.*

26. The Spanish court was at Vallodolid in the early years of the seventeenth century. Cervantes was summoned there in 1603, in connection with his debt to the government.

27. The three quotations from Ovid are, respectively, from the *Ars Amandi*, III, 405–408; from the *Fasti*, VI, 5; and from the *Amores*, III, ix, 17. The translations:

"Poets were once upon a time the concern of kings and leaders, and the choruses of old won for them large prizes; holy was the respect shown to bards and venerable their name, and great wealth frequently was heaped upon them."

"There is a god in us; he stirs and we grow warm."

"And yet we speak of poets as divine, the beloved of the gods."

28. In the original there is a sound play on the verbs *"imitar"* and *"vomitar."*

29. Play on *"trasero,"* meaning "hinder" or "rear" and also "buttock" or "rump." It is the small boy's rump that is his "bondsman."

30. Coaches were notorious as being conducive to libertinism. The coach here is treated as a pimp.

31. Ecclesiasticus 38:1–4. The translation: "Honor the physician out of necessity, for he hath been created by the Almighty; for from God cometh all healing, and from the king he shall receive gifts. The learning of the physician shall lift up his head, and in the presence of the great shall he

be praised. Out of the earth the Almighty hath created medicine, and the wise man will not shun it."

32. "Take upon arising"—literally, "at dawn." The doctor mistakes *"diluculo"* for a drug.

33. Almost untranslatable word play on *"salir,"* meaning "to go out," "go forth," and also "to attain one's objective."

34. The degree of licentiate was intermediate between that of bachelor and doctor.

35. This was a legal privilege of the order and of other similar ones concerned with the ransoming of captives.

36. *"Banco"*—"bench," also means "a money-changer," who sat on a bench to receive and pay out money.

37. *"Cuento"* is "a story" and also signifies "a million." The Genoese were noted for their fleecing of Spaniards.

38. The character of this game is uncertain.

39. In connection with this, it is of interest to compare the views on censorship of the theater set forth in *Don Quixote*, Part I, Chapter LVIII, and the portrait of the puppet master in Part II, Chapters XXV–XXVII.

40. The *"hidalgo"*—"gentleman," was originally the "son of a somebody." Cervantes employs the form that indicates this: *"hijodalgo."*

41. *"Nemo"* is Latin for "no one," "no man." By using the word as a proper noun and employing it in a number of well-known quotations, the licentiate gives them an affirmative instead of a negative sense. The passages cited are from Matthew 11:27; the school text *Disticha catonis*, verse 10; Horace's *Satires*, I, 1–3; and John 3:13. Glasscase read: "Nemo knoweth the Father; Nemo lives without offense; Nemo is content with his lot; Nemo hath ascended up to heaven."

42. Play on the Portuguese verbs meaning "to have" and "to dye." Glasscase addresses the man in bad Portuguese.

43. Swearing by the beard was a common form of oath.

44. Reference to the story of Naaman the leper, in II Kings 5.

45. Nitric acid.

46. *"Por la pinta y por la tinta."*

47. Play on the verb *"murmurar,"* in the sense of hum, and *"murmurador,"* "detractor" or "slanderer."

48. Ecclesiasticus 10:5: "The prosperity of man is in the hand of God, and on the face of the scribe he imposeth honor." (The Vulgate has *"prosperitas hominis,"* not *"potestas hominis."*)

49. Vallodolid was noted for the mud of its streets and its foggy weather.

50. That is, it would have been better if she had died.

51. I Chronicles 16:22: "Touch not mine anointed."

52. See Pliny's *Natural History*, X, 3.

53. *"Juegos de estocada."* A number of card games are mentioned here,

but as Rodríguez Marín observes, no one any longer knows how they were played.

54. "*Rueda*" is a "wheel."

55. Play on "*seguir*"—"to follow," and "*perseguir*"—"to persecute."

THE COLLOQUY OF THE DOGS

The text is that of the first edition, as given in Schevill and Bonilla's *Obras Completas*. For the notes I have drawn upon Rodríguez Marín and upon the special edition of the *novela* by Agustín G. de Amezúa y Mayo.

1. I have seen fit to render "*coloquio*" by the English "colloquy" rather than "dialogue" or "conversation." (I have employed "dialogue" in the subtitle.) According to the dictionary, a colloquy is "mutual discourse: especially a somewhat formal conference," and this seems to convey the idea. "Mahudes" has not been identified.

2. Cervantes' birthplace.

3. "*Salí un águila en esto*"—literally, "became an eagle at this (compare our "ace").

4. The meat days ("*días de carne*") were all the days of the week except Friday and Saturday and special feast days or the eves of such feasts.

5. There is an untranslatable word play here: "*criadas con criadillas*"—"servant maids with lamb cutlets."

6. The calle de la Caza was the street where the game merchants kept shop; the Costanilla, or Slope, was the site of the Fish Market; the Matadero was the municipal slaughter house.

7. The proverbial expression was "*del lobo un pelo y ése de la frente*"—"a hair of the wolf and that from the forehead," the sense being, according to Maccoll, "get what you can from an ugly customer."

8. Expression used in calling a dog.

9. Allusion to the ancient custom (mentioned by Pliny) of spitting in the presence of danger or by way of averting an evil spell.

10. "*A la jineta.*"

11. Name given to a bull or a dog white in color with brown or red spots.

12. Allusion to the first satire of Juvenal, verse 30: "*Difficile est satyram non scribere . . .*"

13. Reference to religious confraternities. The "brothers of light" marched in processions, carrying tapers; the "brothers of blood" were flagellants.

14. Allusion to *La Arcadia* of Lope de Vega.

15. See the first part of Cervantes' *La Galatea*.

16. The reference is to *El Pastor de Fílida* of Luis Gálvez de Montalvo (Madrid, 1582).

17. See the well-known work by Jorge de Montemayor, *Los Siete Libros de la Diana* (Valencia, 1559 ?).

18. *"Deum de Deo"* is from the liturgy ("God of God"). *"De donde diere"* is nonsensical ("I gave whence I shall give"). As for the Academy of Imitators, there was an actual Academia Imitatoria at Madrid, founded for the purpose of imitating the writers of Italy.

19. *"De aquella marina."* The meaning of *"marina"* is in some doubt.

20. A song mentioned by Lope de Vega and others.

21. Allusion to the peacock.

22. See note 61 below.

23. *"Jugar los cubiletes y la agallas."* This is, literally, our shell game.

24. *"Para poner en un monumento sobre panos negros."* I have expanded here on *"monumento."*

25. *"Sobre los estribos ha de andar"*—"up in the stirrups."

26. As Rodríguez Marín observes, the author appears to forget that it is a dog speaking.

27. *"Echemos pellilos a la mar."* Proverbial formula for reconciliation.

28. That is, to Jesus. Rodríguez Marín also finds this remark out of place.

29. That is, Latin grammars. Allusion to the *Introductiones Latinae* of Antonio de Nebrija (Salamanca, 1481). This text was in use until the nineteenth century.

30. That hunger and the itch were indeed the schoolboy's constant companions is attested by others writers.

31. *"Razón de estado."*

32. Compare Dante's *Inferno*, Canto V, verses 121–23.

33. *"Vareatados con sus listas de latin"*—literally, with their stripes, or streaks, of Latin.

34. The octopus's arms (as we say) were called *"rabos,"* but Cipión terms them *"colas." "Cola"* means "tail" and *"rabo"* means "tail end" or "backside." The latter word was regarded as offensive.

35. The anecdote is from Valerius Maximus, VI, 5.

36. "He has the ox on his tongue." On this proverb, see the *Adages* of Erasmus.

37. *"Mi perra."* It was the custom to refer to slaves as *"perros"*—"dogs."

38. "Breton" is here used in the sense of foreigner.

39. Traveling light, usually with only the clothes they wore on their backs, the "Bretons" were noted for their lack of cleanliness.

40. The phrase in the original is *"unto y bisunto,"* an Italianism (*unto e bisunto*), signifying "smeared with oil" or "greasy."

41. Italian for "gold crowns."

42. *"Toda la chirinola desta historia." "Chirinola"* is argot for a band of thieves or ruffians (Rodríguez Marín).

43. The landlady says "*a perpenan rei de memoria*" for "*ad perpetuam rei memoriam*," the phrase used in the patent of nobility.

44. She means, "I'm no lynx."

45. To the "*asistente*." The "*asistente*" was the chief officer of justice at Seville.

46. What Cervantes is discussing here is lawyers, or the legal profession.

47. The Colegio-Universidad de Santa María de Jésus, founded by Rodrigo Fernández de Santaella in the latter half of the fifteenth century.

48. As Rodríguez Marín notes, the reference to the licentiate Sarmiento de Valladares, who was *asistente* of Seville in 1589, tends to show that the action in this part of the story takes place about the time when Cervantes was engaged in the task of requisitioning supplies for the Invincible Armada and frequently resided in Seville.

49. The Sauceda incident calls for a word of explanation. Sauceda was a stretch of pasture land, more than sixteen leagues in extent, in the heart of the inaccessible Ronda highlands. Certain criminal elements from the army took refuge there some time after 1570. Their number increased constantly, and efforts to subdue them were unavailing. It was not until twenty years later that the colony was dissolved after a royal pardon had been granted, representing in reality a capitulation on the part of the government. The allusion to the "destruction" of Sauceda is therefore probably ironical.

50. This was Monipodio's house, described in "Rinconete and Cortadillo."

51. The horse of Gnaeus Sejus, mentioned by Aulus Gellius (III, 9), that brought bad luck to all its owners. The Romans had a proverb: "*Ille homo habet equum Sejanum*"—"That man has the Sejan horse." See the *Adages* of Erasmus.

52. Proverbial expression.

53. Reference to Mairena del Alcor. There is a Mairena del Aljarafe, which is nearer Seville.

54. Blind men and mountebanks were in the habit of teaching their dogs to leap "for the King of France" or "the good tavernkeeper's wife," but not for "the Turk" or "the churlish landlady." See the third act of Lope de Vega's *La Noche Toledana*.

55. "My lady Pimpinel of Paphlagonia" (the drummer says "Dona Pimpinela de Plafagonia") is a burlesque name. The hostelry of Valdeastillas was a famous one.

56. Cervantes gives the name Passillas to the under-sacristan in his interlude *La Guarda Cuidadosa* (see "The Picket of Love" in S. Griswold Morley's translation of the *Entremeses*).

57. Literally, a senate ("*senado*"); the expression was commonly employed by puppet masters and strolling players.

58. The text reads "more than sixty"—"*más de sesenta años.*" Inasmuch as the old woman, a little later, states that she is seventy-five, I have adopted Rodríguez Marín's emendation.

59. See note 61 below.

60. The Thessalian Erichtho (mentioned by the poet Lucan) was famous for her knowledge of medicines and poisons.

61. There were a number of women known as the Camachas of Montilla. According to information gleaned by editor Amezúa, one of them, whose right name was Leonor Rodríguez, was living in the town in 1573. (Note that Montiela's lover is "Rodríguez the laborer.") She was tried by the Holy Office of Cordova. The term "*las Camachas*" came to be applied not only to her but to her companions and disciples as well. Among the crimes of which the Camachas were accused was that of having transformed Don Alonso de Aguilar, son of the Marquis of Priego, into a horse. There is also more than one legend that tells of a woman giving birth to puppies. The ability to grow roses in December (p. 176) was another common attribute of witches, and the headless horse, or devil's mount (p. 191), as the author indicates, frequently figured in fireside conversations. The truth is, the belief in witchcraft was an old one in Spain. Henry Charles Lea, in *A History of the Inquisition in Spain* (New York, 1907; Vol. IV, pp. 206–207), dates it from the middle of the fourteenth century and finds that it was increased by persecution; it had virtually disappeared by the end of the eighteenth century. Professor Schevill describes the Lea work as a basic one for the subject; but allowance always is to be made for the author's intense Protestant bias.

62. Compare the prophecy of Anchises in the sixth book of the Aeneid: "*Parcere subiectis et debellare superbos.*"

63. It is of interest to note that Cervantes here finds an opportunity to broach his favorite theme, that of the illusory and the real.

64. On Cañizares's defense of hypocrisy, see what Aubrey Bell, in his *Cervantes* (Norman: University of Oklahoma Press, 1947; p. 173), has to say, by way of refuting Américo Castro.

65. "*El nombre de las fiestas*" literally, "the name of feast days," it being the custom, at Eastertide and on the occasion of other feasts, for pastors to accuse their parishioners of the sins the latter had committed. The phrase had come to be associated with the idea of recrimination or censure.

66. These are proverbs.

67. See note 61.

68. Referring to the ecclesiastical change of hoods.

69. There was a comedy bearing this title; it is mentioned by Quevedo. Daraja is a character in the Moorish romances and in the novelette that is introduced in the first part of the *Guzmán de Alfarache*.

70. Raisin stems were supposed to be good for the memory.

71. These appear to be real persons, though not much is known about them.

72. Horace says nine years, not ten (*Ars Poetica*, 386–89).

73. The text has "*demanda del Santo Brial*"—literally, "quest of the Holy Skirt"; a play on "*brial*"—"a silken skirt," and "*grial*"—"grail." Or could it be a typographical error?

74. The point of longitude for mariners, a problem that troubled sixteenth-century navigators.

75. Schevill cites E. W. Hobson's *Squaring the Circle: A History of the Problem* (Cambridge University Press, 1913).

76. Expression often used for emphasis.

77. Somewhat redundant.

78. "*Pareceles a vuesas mercedes que sería barro*"—"do you think it is mud?" Compare our slang expression with regard to a considerable sum of money: "that ain't hay."

79. Cervantes himself, it is to be remembered, had been a commissary.

80. "*Alcalde*."